I0669149

YOU WOUND ME

Copyright © 2026 by Alair Novak

All rights reserved. No part of this book may be used or reproduced to train Artificial Intelligence (AI) in any manner whatsoever without written permission from Alair Novak. This work is not to be reproduced, translated in any other language, or used for monetary purposes whatsoever without written permission except in the case of brief quotations embodied in critical articles, reviews, or self-use social media content.

This book is a work of fiction. Names, characters, businesses, organizations, places, events, and incidents either are the product of the author's imagination or are used fictitiously. Any resemblance to actual persons, living or dead, events, or locales is entirely coincidental. Additionally, any advice and opinions contained in this book do not always reflect the author's opinion and may not be suitable for your situation. The author shall not be liable for any damages, including but not limited to special, incidental, consequential, personal, or other damages.

Cover Design: Alair Novak
Formatting: Designs by Kage
Chapter art: Designs by Kage
Editing: Jessica Snoots & Roxana Coumans

First Edition : January 2026
ISBN : 979-8-9918060-3-9

AUTHORS NOTE

Hello inmate, I'm writing this in fall of 2025, following Pride month, Men's Mental Health month, and major U.S. holidays. This book is due January of 2026 which, as many of us know, is very challenging for some readers.

Having worked in the medical field for thirteen years, I've seen my fair share of declined health, suicide attempts, increased mental health cases, even more so now that I work as a Correctional Officer. In addition, I have many family members who work in Law Enforcement, the military, and other areas of the medical field. Therefore, we do not take mental health lightly here—not in this house.

Moving forward, although *You Wound Me* is a work of fiction, the contents affect normal everyday people like you and myself. I understand a lot of people read to escape the realities of their lives, but I write for readers to relate and have representation for their own illnesses. That said, this is a romantic tragedy and will hurt your feelings. I shed light on this because losing loved ones is never easy, especially during winter.

My team and I want to extend our love to you through this time of year.

Whether you're fighting internal battles, struggling financially, healing from the loss of a family member, dealing with the fall out of a tragic event, or simply feeling lost with no way to find sunlight—you are in our hearts.

If you ever need to seek help, I have provided contact information to reputable sources if you're in fear of your life or have no one to turn to. I promise there is someone who will listen and hear your story.

National Sexual Assault Hotline
1-800-656-5673 (call & text)

Suicide and Crisis Lifeline
988 (call & text)

Battle Buddy Response Team
855-777-2278

CopLine
800-267-5463

The Trevor Project
1-866-488-7386

Text START to 678-678

Trans Lifeline
1-877-565-8860

National Runaway Safeline
1-800-RUNAWAY

Playlist

Riders on the Storm - The Doors

Cold as Ice - Foreigner

Heartbreaker - Led Zeppelin

Ready for Love - Bad Company

House of Broken Love - Great White

Slow an' Easy - Whitesnake

Stairway to Heaven - Led Zeppelin

What You Give - Tesla

Stranglehold - Ted Nugent

Stop Draggin' My Heart Around - Stevie Nicks, Tom Petty and the Heartbreakers

Young Lust - Pink Floyd

Up All Night - Slaughter

What Do You Want from Me - Pink Floyd

Shot in the Dark - Ozzy Osbourne

Planet Caravan - Black Sabbath

Fire Woman - The Cult

Don't Know What You Got - Cinderella

I'm The Only One - Melissa Etheridge

Burnin' for You - Blue Oyster Cult

ALAIR NOVAK

Sweet Emotion - Aerosmith
Ramble On - Led Zeppelin
Bringin' On The Heartbreak - Def Leppard
When the Levee Breaks - Led Zepplin
For Those About to Rock - AC/DC
I Can Love You Like That - John Michael Montgomery
Wish You Were Here - Pink Floyd
Hey Hey, My My - Nightcore
Owner of a Lonely Heart - Yes

To the forever young,
Your memory will live on in the eyes of those who thought the world of
you.
Rest in peace all* those who we have lost.

Charles, Jay, Jonathan, Shayna, Valkyrie, Kandi, Leonard, Kyle, Ashlee, Stephanie, Lela, TJ, Jaclyn, Ralph, Dennis, Alvie, Shaun, Richard, Charlotte, Janet, Zelma, Les, Bobby, Tonya, Roberta, Chris, Sue, Doug, Jeff, Peggy, George, Mikey, Scott, Tom & countless others.

WARNING

The content of this book is for mature audiences only. Themes inside include erotic scenes and criminal behavior, which are not suitable for audiences under the age of 18.

Additionally, I'm not an expert on criminal activity or street racing. I ask you to take errors with a grain of salt. *You Wound Me* is a work of fiction and some family dynamics within this book are not suitable for real life comparisons.

Tropes

First everything, criminal mischief, romantic tragedy, friends to lovers, star-crossed lovers, small town romance, high school sweethearts, adrenaline junkie, emotional read.

Trigger/Content Warning

Major character death, angst, grief & loss, criminal mischief, underage alcohol use, underage drug use, mentions of family abuse, speeding & unsafe driving.

This is a romantic tragedy.

Your mental health matters. Proceed at your own risk.

Word From The MMC

Hello reader, this is your MMC speaking. Before we slide into *You Wound Me*, Alair wants me to spend a moment with you. As you can see, you didn't get any details for my book. You don't have chapter names, you weren't told who your MC's are, but you were warned this book will not end on a HEA.

This isn't quite a prologue, but it's all I can do to prevent you from moving forward if you're not feeling well mentally. You won't find things like sexual assault, murder, or mental health representation in *You Wound Me*, but you will find heartache. You will see our lives from my POV, experience my emotions, my love for the FMC, and witness how proud of her I am. You will also experience the grief associated with loss and no true coping mechanisms outside of self-isolation, self-doubt and substance use.

Moving forward, *You Wound Me* is being released during winter where there are increased numbers of suicide, suicide ideation, accidental death, murder, and self-harm. If you cannot handle your heart being broken, please close the book and come back when the sun is warm and you have a support system ready to help you battle your demons. While it's not my intention to harm you, the title will make sense in the end.

Alright, sweetheart.
Let's go for a ride.

CHAPTER ONE

"Dios mio, Kaleb! Qué auga tan caliente!"

Shit!

"Lo siento, mamá!" I shout back. The thin bathroom door and the hiss of shower water drown out the bass of my low timbre. The sound rumbling deep in my chest, even if she doesn't quite hear me.

That's my mom though—admonishing me for using too much of the hot water. We're limited; water heaters don't hold much anymore so we burn through it pretty quick in this old house. The torrent is already beginning to cool, steam thickening around me as the temperature from my blazing skin and the colder water struggle to mix.

In all honesty, I should have jumped out of the shower long ago, but shit happens. Doesn't take much for me to get sidetracked when I don't have something for my hands to tinker with, such as the frustrating fucking turbo I've spent all day trying to install in the Civic. At first I couldn't get the intake to attach. Then I scraped the absolute hell out of the knuckles on my right hand when my greasy grip slipped off the wrench and slammed

1

into the exhaust manifold. They split wide open, poured blood all over the damn place and are currently mocking me while I bathe.

Puffy and angry skin burns when the slowly-cooling water cascades over them, add in soap and they're practically screaming for relief that's not coming any time soon. They're annoying but moving around them is what's keeping me distracted—partially. What's really haunting me is a pair of silver eyes that have done nothing but consume my dreams and flit through my thoughts when I'm least expecting it.

My heart doesn't act right either, when I get to thinking about them, pounding ferociously in my chest, catching my breath between the fluttering muscles. Seeing her, thinking of her, and racing; they pump so much adrenaline into my bloodstream I live in a constant high.

Tonight's the night, though. I'm going to see my girl for the first time in a handful of years–two to be exact. The last time I saw her? My graduation. She still had a baby face but doesn't anymore. How do I know? Well, my homie Logan has been after her friend for a while and spends many of his weekends at our other buddy's house. When they do hang out, he sneaks Polaroids and shows them to me back on campus—sometimes my girl is in them and when she's not, I turn a blind eye. Needless to say, the photos with her in them come up missing every time. I like to think he knows I'm stealing them, but I'll never admit to it.

Having ten sticky fingers is the lesser of my crimes, but we all know nothing is illegal unless you get caught. Good luck nailing me to the cross; the police aren't quite fast enough yet—maybe one day.

That's the effect she has on me by the way—turns me into one dumb motherfucker. Chopping my thoughts up into millions of little pieces too emulsified to be distinguished from another. Pure idiocy. When it comes to her, I struggle to figure out where one thought ends and the next begins.

Don't get me started on time either. It melds together, the seconds, minutes, and hours, there one second then *poof*—gone in a cloud of rich exhaust. Next thing I know, I'm still knee deep in my damn head and have fucked up something else on the car. Can't tell you how many times I've had to start something over all because I was daydreaming like a love drunk fool.

Things have been like this since the day we met. The memory is still so fresh I can hear the chattering of the lunchroom in the back of my mind. It was my junior year, and she was a freshman; tension was high, the air a little testy, and students were moving around all shifty like. That's when I caught eye of what was happening when I spotted the devilish girl absolutely wailing on someone.

Before the coaches could step in, I swooped over, wrapped an arm around her waist, and jerked her back as the victim lay crying and bleeding—scrambling back with gratitude. She held my attention for point two seconds before I was focused on the writhing typhoon in my arms, fighting me in order to get back to her target.

I held on tight to the whirlwind, eventually getting to see who I was holding captive but not after a few new bumps and bruises of my own.

"Woah killer! Relax!"

"If you know what the hell's good for you, you'll let me go!"

Her voice is breathy, a little on the lower side—unlike the rest of the girls in our school—and laced with so much disdain it makes me laugh.

"I'm not too bright. Why don't you tell me what will happen if I don't, hmm?"

Zero hesitation, she's wheels around and gives me not just a piece of her mind but the whole fucking cake.

"I'll beat your ass next, hotshot. There's not a single one of you in this school that scares me—especially some half-sacked jock. Now kick rocks, goon."

Before she can escape me—because let's be honest. That little jab hurt a smidge—I grab and drag her back to me. Both of my hands, calloused thanks to football and my needy car, cup her furious face; still pink with anger and a few cat-fight scratches. What I'm met with sucks the breath out of my lungs and I forget where I'm at, what I'm doing, who I am.

The sharpest pair of sterling-grey eyes, molten in their anger, meet my roasted-coffee toned ones. Fucking hell, she's beautiful.

"What's your name, Diabolica?"

She scowls, hands instantly finding and shoving at my chest—her enthusiasm barely ruffling the buttery-leather of my worn-out jacket. When I don't release her, the coaches scraping her victim off the floor to our left, she softens. Inhaling the longest calming breath I've ever seen.

"Nadia."

I don't know if she's ever realized how much power she has over me, but ever since that day, her hooks have been buried deep into my skin—barbed, bone scraping hooks. Then, if I moseyed too far away, the mere mention of her name would drag me right back to where I belong—her side.

Anyway, you can bet your fine ass I'm not going to confess any of this to her—she'd use it against me for fun. I can't have that when I'm trying to sweep little miss viciousness off her feet and cart her back to the city with me.

A quick shake of my head flings water all throughout the steamy shower. Obsidian strands snap to my forehead in an array of directions and patterns the movement wafting the stall with the lemony-bergamot scent of my Drakkar Nior shampoo. I've used this brand since high school for very obvious reasons. Ma was given a bottle as a white elephant gift during a Christmas potluck dinner at an old job. She didn't want to be rude and give it to someone else, the thought of having another man's shampoo in her bathroom since my dad disappeared hurt too much, so she gave it to me instead.

I wasn't going to use it either, but when Ma lost her job, we were low on money and I was out of my normal brand. You wouldn't catch me dead smelling foul, I had to do what I had to do.

At that time I was already seeing Nadia—if that's what you want to call it—we had been dating in our own way for a few months. You know, typical teenage type dates: football games, skating rinks, diner drive-ins; nothing extravagant for two broke as hell kids. It was how easy I caught her attention the first day I approached her lunch table wearing the Drakkar. She followed my every move, assessing me like a predator ready to eat me whole. That day I knew it would always be my favorite scent. After practice that day, she shoved her tongue so far down my throat I nearly needed the Heimlich—I've used it ever since.

With the water clear of my eyes now, I fist my bar of soap and lather it up with a washcloth until globs of suds plopped on the floor. It's rich and creamy across my pecan-toned skin as I scrub away the dirt and grime from hours upon hours working on the car. Focused on my hands and arms, the cloth roughs up the filth staining my flesh—a few specks that mimic freckles finally smear away and rise off when I step beneath the raining shower head.

House of Broken Love begins to whine at full volume through the AM/FM radio. Honestly, it's a wonder I heard Ma at all—yelling through the flimsy door about the limited hot water supply. Tipping my head, the torrent streams over me in rivulets as the crying guitar fades out and the disk jockey's voices over the remaining notes.

"That, ladies and gents, is *the* Great White. Did you know the band was initially called Dante Fox? Their manager suggested they change to Great White in reference to their guitarist, Mark. All due to his white-blond hair, white wardrobe, and his BC Rich guitar. Anyway, folks, it's the top of the hour. Get ready for a full sixty minutes of non-stop classic hits."

Fuck me, I'm going to be late!

Wrenching the hot and cold water valves off—the last few dribbles of water spluttering from the shower head and splat on dull chrome-plated faucet with a harsh *ting*. The next song loads up as I yank the curtain back, plastic rings rake across the top of the shower rod, disrupting the screaming whammy of *Stranglehold*. Humid air outside of the stall, several degrees cooler than what was surrounding me just seconds ago, splashes across me like ice, causing me to shiver with chills racing down my arms and legs.

Whisking a towel off one of the hooks hanging on the outside of the stall, I lug one around my hips and tie it loosely; the itchy fibers, more polyester than cotton, refuse to absorb the water droplets. Instead they begin combining, dripping down my legs and stomach, tickling the sparse hairs connecting my belly button to my pelvis.

Padding to the small vanity, I nearly slip when my wet foot misses the crumpled bathroom mat, and practically catapults out from under me.

"FUCK!"

I shit you not—my soul ejecto-seatoed and went for a quick run around the damn equator before slamming back into my body. Grappling, I catch the ceramic sink and steady myself, almost knocking the radio off the counter along with the clothes I had tossed on top. Never mind my worn-out boots which are now crushed against the door jam from my sudden home run slide.

Once I'm finally dressed in a pair of boot-cut jeans, a black t-shirt, and an open dark grey button-up, I saunter into Ma's kitchen. The weathered rubber of my shoes thud along the worn carpet before the floor abruptly transitions to linoleum. Despite the obsessive cleaning Ma does, the plastic coating still has that slightly sticky sound and feeling under my soles.

Snagging the backrest of a kitchen table chair, I whirl it around and drop into a straddle, giving a slight wiggle to get comfortable. Crossing my arms along the top, bracing myself, I glance and salivate over the spread she's cooked up. The aromas are spicy, earthy, and sublime. A mix of fresh veggies fried up with garlic and lemon—I'll never get tired of her cooking. We may not have much, but Ma makes sure we eat like there's no tomorrow.

"About time you got your ass out of that shower and showed your face."

That's Uncle Ren, Lorenzo, or Officer Reyes depending on the day. Other than my sisters Camilla and Ximena, he's the only family we have left. For some fucked up reason, he decided to start acting like our father instead of our uncle. Instead of showing his smug face at our dinner table every damn day, I wish he would put more of his effort into playing with the badge-bunnies at his precinct than being here—they actually want his time whereas we wish he didn't exist.

Hearing his pissy attitude, it's safe to assume he's going by Officer Reyes today rather than Uncle, but the five-o isn't my friend, and neither is Uncle Ren. Dickead cherishes his corroded badge and oppressive brotherhood more than his own flesh and blood. He chooses to shun the very people he grew up with—those who had protected him and gave the shifts off their back on more than one occasion. Now he looks at them over the barrel of a gun and refuses to listen rather than shout. One day Karma will come around and he will be spoon fed his just desserts with the same kind of contempt.

Unfortunately, Ma loves the hell out of him. That's her brother, the baby of eight of them, so I suppose she has to but that doesn't mean I do. So, like the pain in the ass I am for him specifically, I don't.

Something tells me he's here for a reason, and I have a sneaking suspicion it's because I'm back in town. I've been chased by cops in the city on more than one occasion. I wouldn't doubt his visit has something to do with that since I, obviously, slip out of their grubby, pig-fingers. Cities and counties talk, they also reach out to the state, so I wouldn't be surprised if they told him they're looking for me and my crew and got word we would be in Hazelwood tonight. Time wasted on this part, even if we're all here they have nothing other than speculation and whispers—that won't hold up in a court of law.

Either way, today is supposed to be a good day—not one where I'm forced to listen to his lectures because my padre is MIA.

Not your shoes to fill, motherfucker.

A fact he has yet to learn and from how things are going, he may never. We're not his fucking kids though, hell half the time I'm not his nephew either and if it wasn't for Ma, we wouldn't be civil with one another. Her feelings get hurt when we start going after one another, but if he wants to poke at me then I'll stab right back then apologize to her later.

Shifting my stare away from the plate of fresh tortillas, grilled carne asada, and elote, I offer him a scowl. If he wants to throw down then I'm game, it's been a while since my knuckles have met something other than the unforgiving surface of my manifold.

"Is that what you come here for? Wallow in our business and stick your snout where it doesn't belong?" I follow up with an obnoxious *'sooie'*.

"Kaleb. No pelees con tu tio," Ma clips.

Don't fight with him; she says.

Whatever. He shouldn't start shit when he knows I'm not one to back down. Scowling, I eventually rip my glare away from Uncle Ren and meet Ma's tender smile. I refuse to let this goober ruin my high. Between the happiness she wears on her lovely face, and knowing I'll get to see Nadia tonight, I'll be damned if I let him rain on my fucking parade.

"Lo siento, madre."

"Where are you going this late? I thought you were staying for dinner?" she asks.

"A party. I missed Nadia's graduation earlier. Since she's going to be out with her friends later, I want to see her."

"That girl's bad news," Ren butts in, waving his fork around.

What kind of Latino eats carne asada and tortillas with a damn fork?

"No one asked for your opinion, pig."

"Doesn't mean I won't share it."

"Hermano, don't antagonize him."

"Ahhh, madre. El credo no me molesta."

"Watch your fucking mouth, Kaleb."

This asshole.

"You've gone so far off the rails, you're abandoning your heritage. Do you not understand Spanish anymore?"

"That's beside the point," he snaps at me.

Instead of goading him more, I shake my head and grab some food—the carne's my favorite. I hate Ma likely made my favorite meal and thought I was going to be her little boy tonight, only to already have plans. Ones I refuse to forgo. Not this time. Maybe in the future.

Ripping some of the perfectly seasoned and grilled meat into bite size pieces, I toss it on a warmed corn tortilla and inhale it. The flavors explode across my tastebuds, making me more ravenous than I already was. As I hurriedly scarf down my food, my right leg begins to bounce with anticipation and anxiety. I get to see her, not in pictures or through word of mouth, actually lay my eyes on her. Three, no four—hell, I don't remember how many tortillas later, I'm pushing away from my seat. Righting the chair and sliding it under the particle board-like table, I lean over and give Ma a kiss on the top of her grey-streaked, black hair. This woman is one of the best things to ever happen to me, even if I can't stick around tonight.

"Volveré más trade. Te amo."

"We're in the United States. Speak English, boy."

Ma swings her kitchen towel at him, hitting the ass in the face, knowing he's intentionally antagonizing me to make me lash out. For someone who wanted to play 'daddy,' he sure is a terrible influence. Once upon a time, our family would have been proud to have a police officer among us. Showing other families coming to the states was the smartest thing we could do to escape the increasing violence in Mexico. Unfortunately, we traded one tyrant for another. Being his kin is an embarrassment.

"Ten cuidado, mijo."

"Si mamá."

Ten. Ten long strides and I'm out of the kitchen into the too-small living room.

By the door sits a catch-all shelf where we drop all of our stuff the moment we walk in, keys, wallets, bags, jackets, you name it. Typically our keys go on a hook on the wall but mine are sitting in a bowl that I promptly snatch them out of. I don't waste time stepping onto the small porch just outside of the trailer door, my clinking metal keys announcing my leave.

I'm not embarrassed of what we have, more so I'm angry over it. Ma deserves better. She used to tell me stories of where our family came from—homes with dirt floors and having to fetch water every morning just to have something to drink while others worked. But she's a godsend of a woman, always pushing me to be the best man I can be and support me in any way she could. She would go out of her way to attend every one of my school events and stop by to have lunch with me occasionally. She bust her ass working extra shifts to pay for my football gear, only to turn around and do it again so my sisters could have the things they wanted too. A trailer house in a run-down park isn't quite the castle she deserves, she loves it.

The day my racing career takes off, I'm putting her in a real home. The kind with solid walls and bricks on the outside, a yard where she can plant a vegetable garden and relax on one of those fancy swing sets with the canopy over it. She will want for nothing, all because she's the mother I was blessed with.

Stomping down the rickety porch steps, the greying wood and rusted nails groaning under my weight, I clear the bottom one with a slight pep in my step. I get to see Nadia, feel her in my damn hands, smell that honey-like scent she always has—drawing me in like a siren.

At my driver-side door, the key grinds when I shove it into the keyhole and turn, the lock clunks free right as I pull the door's latch. Inside, pre-summer warmth and sun has heated the stock steering wheel, center console, and the leather back seats to the point it permeates the air and slaps me in the face. Though she's a mean bitch, I love this damn car.

Sliding into the driver seat, the key feeds into the ignition; she purrs to life with a loud growl that reverberates off the trailer next to ours. Pink Floyd joins in, flooding the cab with music so loud it vibrates the plastic housings shielding the speakers—almost as good as the real thing.

Shifting her into reverse, I reach for the left shoulder of the passenger seat and brace myself. Diligently looking out the rear window, I clear the short driveway and avoid Officer Reyes's ugly fucking cruiser that's parked too close for my liking. He invades everything, like some sort of Spanish conquistador.

How hard is it to give people room to back out of their parking spots?

The road out of here squeezes narrowly between other trailers making it a hazard to drive down since kids race up and down the street on their bicycles, hooting and hollering from supper happiness. They don't have a sidewalk so they make do with what they have, I don't blame them. It's a simple joy. Pushing in the clutch and shifting into drive, we launch forward, erupting the park with growls that rattle windows and surely piss off my uncle.

Tonight's the night.

I've missed my delinquent for far too long, now it's time to steal her away.

CHAPTER TWO

Three days ago

"**M**an, come on! We have shit to do!" I shout at my boys. They're too busy messing around with the freshmen girls instead of having their head in the damn game.

Our last class finished about twenty minutes ago—finals are over—and I'm ready to get out of here. There's only so much of this school I can take, especially when I can't stand being here in the first place. College wasn't my dream, it's my mom's. She wants more for me, preferably an education beyond high school unlike the rest of my family—and her, which she never points out.

"There's more for you, mi hijo." She likes to remind me, when side eyeing my two friends. Don't get me started on what she thinks of them. I know they're problem children too but you know what they always say, birds of a feather. Not to toot my own horn but I'm the better influence, so it's up to me to corral them like livestock when there are things to get done.

I gave them time to fuck around but now I want to be on the blacktop, not on campus. There's asphalt and rubber to burn, spilled oil, high octane fuel, wind whipping past me ruffling my hair, a beautiful woman on my arm, maybe a little bit of fame? Life in the fast lane and nothing less.

Racing is my passion—the career path I'm aiming for with every ounce of effort. Not this collegiate bullshit; collared polos, khaki shorts, and seashell necklaces. I crave leather and fishnets, parties, and rock 'n roll that never sleeps.

While I'm here to appease my mom, you bet your sweet ass I still get race time. Matter of fact, there's a race in a few days I'm dying to join in on but it interferes with a much more important graduation party.

Hazelwood is a shit hole but it's alright. Remember that beautiful woman I was talking about wanting on my arm? She's who I'm really going home to see.

Nadia Rayle Pierce.

Miss resident bully-ass kicker who doesn't take no for an answer, fights her way through people twice her size, and lets nothing stand in her way. Could say she's the full fucking package and I'd argue she's more than that in every way. I like to think no one has a clue how obsessed I am with her, not even the devil himself, but I am. Every move I have made since leaving home has been to build a future with her—and my racing career, let's be honest. It's my job to provide for the both of us, especially now that she's legally an adult aching to ditch Hazelwood for good. Whatever it takes to get her away from her sorry excuse of a father—even if that means suffering through boring lectures and one hundred question final exams for my mom.

Nonetheless, college can suck it. There are better things to do, bags to pack, speed limits to break—all so I can claim the girl I've been after for years. As soon as these numb nuts figure out their head from their ass.

"Ahh, Kaleb. Buzz off!" Wesley blurts.

"Nah, you can chase tail when we get back. There's plenty to go around."

"Speak for yourself, bro. Not everyone has pussy sitting at home waiting around. Gotta get what we can, ya know what I mean?" He teases me this time. Rubbing his patchy facial hair and still thin jawline. Always trying to impress girls who want nothing to do with him. Other than Nadia, Wesley's my oldest friend; with half a brain, he gets half a name—Wes the mess.

He thinks he's hot shit but he's at the bottom of our class and usually last to the finish line too—only hanging around for the race-bunnies. He's a good dude though, I guess. If I ever need him in a pinch, he's there. Financial aid didn't post? He covers my tuition until it does. Assholes in one of my electives trying to start shit they can't back up? He's there. Need alcohol and still haven't turned twenty-one? Whatever brand you want, he will supply it.

All of that loyalty and the dumb ass just got out of lockup. He keeps going the same route he will lose his scholarship and will have to go back to paying for school out of his gold-lined pockets. Trust me when I say college is expensive for no damn reason—it's not worth the price tag.

The shithead next to him is Logan, an absolute genius. He helps me with the Civic's computer system and tuneups when he has time. I installed a light-weight sound system a while back, which has done nothing but give me electrical issues since, makes me want to rip out my hair—the components too. Just when you think reading the installation instructions were good enough to get the job done, the shit malfunctions. God forbid something be easy.

Now, put an engine in front of me and I'll have it torn apart, problem found, cleaned, and put back together before the night's done. Zap, that's what we call Logan, would have pieces falling all over the place. Don't get me started on his aversion to grease—he puts his electronics together with gloves on and hooked up to a grounding wire. Apparently, you can kill a motherboard if you have static on your person, who would have thought. After going through all the trouble of installing things, shorting out the computer system would send me off the deep end.

"Where are we going again?" Zap inquires, angling his head where he can look over the rim of his glasses to get a better look at the group idiot.

"Hazelwood, fucker. Those barely eighteen girls out there are ripe for the picking."

"That's disturbing. Don't talk about them like that; that's a good way to get your teeth knocked in." I snap.

"Chill man, your girl's newly eighteen. What's the difference?"

"I've known her for years, there's history there."

"Mmmmhmmm. In that case, they've been waiting for me. Hah!"

The girls he was attempting to swoon narrowly escape when he starts paying more attention to me than them—you're welcome ladies. Hearing the way he talks about Nadia is one thing, but to talk about other girls? Unacceptable. At least mine can fight and would black both his eyes if she heard him speaking this way.

Snapping an arm out, my hand fists the neck of his shirt until the cotton burns my skin, then I yank him to me. Our noses are a hairs breath away as I invade his precious space, about as uncomfortably as he makes other people. He's a few inches shorter than me, along with being a pig, that makes it easy to bully the shithead when needed.

At this proximity, I can almost taste the mouthwash he used this morning, from how hard he breathes—akin to a panting dog. I guess when you call it 'chasing tail' you tend to embody one. What an embarrassment. Snarling, I hold him in place since guys like Wes don't understand the concept of decency unless it comes sandwiched between two slices of violence.

"Mind what you fucking say about her. Nadia's mine and always has been. You're talking about picking up girls simply because they're newly eighteen. That makes you sound like a predator. Is that what your new paint job needs to read? I like my girls groomed? If that's the case, we can always put your head beneath a rear wheel and see how long it spins before I accidentally lose control and rip your fucking face off."

"Woahhhhh, Rey, that's excessive. Come on. He's just a dumb shit. Don't put him in the hospital."

I tilt my head a fraction and watch Wes's eyes snap over to Zap—almost like he's thanking him for stepping in.

There's no way around it, keeping Nadia's name out of their mouths has been a vital part of my tenure here. They don't typically say anything but now that I'm able to finally be with her they're getting ballsy. Can't have that, not when I'm so damn close to having her in my hands.

Shoving him, Wes stumbles back while Zap crosses his arms over and stares at him unimpressed. Me though? I straighten my jacket, the one I wear too often for it being late spring. Call it my safety blanket if you will but it still gets a little chilly when I'm running the roads. It's become a permanent piece of my appearance and until the temperatures reach eighty and above, I'll keep wearing it.

Wes gives me the dirtiest look, throwing both hands up in exasperation as other classmates filter by unaware of the intensity flaring between the three of us. He's red-faced, obviously pissed off for getting man handled in public for one, two…I hurt his ego. There'll be a day where he catches another charge and it will come from shit just like this; saying the wrong thing to the wrong girl in front of the wrong man—idiot.

"You're an asshole, bro. Why you gotta say it like that?"

"What, call you out on your shitty behavior?"

"It was just a comment!"

"That's how it starts. Next you'll be in private messages with little girls."

"Fuck you!"

Zap intervenes again, stepping between us when Wes tries to charge me up. His larger hands land roughly on Wes's shoulders and preventing him from making another dumb ass decision that gets him laid out on the fucking ground.

"Relax, he made his point. Want to prove him wrong? Then do it. Stop saying piggish-things."

"Fuck you too, Zap! Always siding with Rey."

"Not siding with anyone. I don't want to scrape you off the sidewalk. I don't have spare gloves on me and the cops will look at me weird."

Wes bows up and shoves Zap, the last buffer before possibly getting his ass handed to him like he deserves. Stepping up to the plate, I'm ready to go a few rounds with him if he's really itching for a fight. Lucky for him he backs off and waves me off, thinking better than to go down this road.

"I'm out of here—my own crew throwing me under the bus like this? Fuck that."

"The bus is better than jail, knuckle head. Get it together. Now, let's get to the dorms and pack up. I told you we have things to do."

I've done enough waiting the past few years; if they're coming, they better hurry the hell up. My boots hit the sidewalk as I turn toward the dorms, leaving them there until they decide to get with the program and catch up. Zap appears at my side in a few strides with Wes shuffling behind him like some temper wielding pubescent child.

Did I say college is pointless? I mean, you have half-assed accolades but the rest of it is worthless. It's an overly expensive piece of paper that may, or may not, get you where you want to be in life. Never met a professional racer with a college degree—pretty sure most are high school dropouts. Doesn't take a whole lot of ingenuity to press pedals, pop clutches, and downshift. It's the rest of the hard work and dedication you can't learn that makes all the difference.

The trek across campus takes us little to no time, my long strides eating up the pavement like a starved man—in a way I am. Every step gets me closer to Hazelwood, and closer to the only girl I've ever wanted.

An hour later and we're loaded, each of us tossing a single backpack in the trunk along with energy drinks and all the weed we can smoke before we end up blazed. I'm not one for the hard stuff, cocaine, meth, whatever else is floating around but a fat joint does take the edge off. Alcohol is alright too but I don't drink much either. It makes me feel out of control, like nothing around me is moving at the pace I need it to. I like the control and the safety it provides.

After an unpredictable life with an absent father, having control means a whole lot more than what people give it credit for. That's likely why I lead this ragtime bunch. I serve a purpose to people who look up to me, outside of my little sisters who would prefer me to stay out of their business.

My sisters are getting old enough to start dating and don't want big brother ruining their lives by chasing the wrong boys off. It's our culture to marry early and start families but if there is one thing I've taught them growing up, it's that we don't have to follow a culture we may not agree with. The younger one agrees and has told me on more than one occasion she's more interested in women while the other is ready to get married at the ripe age of seventeen.

Over my dead body.

The boy she likes is part of the bike circuit in Detroit. Typical squid, acting cool with a bike that's too big for his skill level. Hangs around in his helmet, makes riding his entire personality, you know prime husband material. Now, I know cars are pretty much my only fall back, but there's more to me than being elbow deep in engine gunk and burning rubber—can't say the same for him.

We've run into one another a few times on the track and he always gets smoked, yet what sets me off the most with him is how often he entertains other girls. In the beginning I told my sister about it but she became defensive and shut me out—I was only doing what was expected of me as a brother, protecting her and all that. Unfortunately, she doesn't see it that way.

Fingers crossed he isn't in Hazelwood this week.

Shrugging off my jacket, I toss it into the back seat next to Zap and drop into the driver's side. I had the Civic fitted with bucket seats in the front so it always feels like I'm ready for race day. There are special fittings underneath to revert back to the stock seats but I prefer the hard-backed ones with five point harnesses instead. Not only are they for me, because this is my car and I'll build her how I want her, but they're also for my passengers. I want them to be safe as well.

Which the guys understand. They don't hesitate to strap in when we go anywhere, letting me know they respect the danger that comes with riding in a car like Delinquent.

While she isn't a drag car, and a roll cage isn't needed, being secure is far better than sitting in a cushy stock seat and having a lower chance of survival.

Exiting campus parking is a task on its own, especially this time of year, so when I finally pull onto the highway I do what I always do and open her up. The torque forces her to bear down a fraction then a second later we're zipping across lanes cutting through traffic with ease.

I love this fucking car, she's so smooth and easy to maneuver. It doesn't take much to glide her from one position to the next, accelerate, or decelerate—she's a hairpin trigger. I built her that way to make racing easier and more effortless as if she's an extension of me and not a machine. Driving on pure instinct and autonomic behavior.

We're several miles down the road once I make it past all the legal drivers, and the ones who should be in the slow lane rather than the first one, before I'm setting the cruise control at a whopping ninety-five. Sitting more comfortably in my seat, I allow my thoughts to drift.

Zap is silent in the back doing whatever on his phone, probably re-searching something to plug into the computer system while Wes is beside me flipping through the radio stations before a song could finish. I find it rather annoying that he never lets one play through but it's better than the bickering—what harm is there anyway?

It's easy to focus on the road when Nadia comes to mind—she lives there, her personal haven deep in my cranium. I don't know if there's enough time but I'd like to take her to see my mom this weekend. It's been a while since they have visited one another and my mom adores the hell out of her. I think she asks about her more than she asks about me when she calls to check in. Rude as hell, especially when I'm the apple of her eye. I'm kidding.

The first time I brought her home, my mom had plates of food piled in front of her, urging her to eat as if she were a stray picked off the road. My abuela is the same way when I visit but between you and me, my mom is this way with Nadia because I opened my mouth one night. There was a time in her childhood when she went without food because her piece of shit father told her it was to learn to cook or starve.

My girl went without food altogether or would choke down the meals she fucked up for weeks, just to have something in her belly. She started with simple things like sandwiches and canned soup but when the supplies ran out, she was left with basic ingredients; throwing away more than what was consumable.

After that, I never let her go without. I even made it a point to take extra food with me in school: tamales, sopes, pozole, or some descada and tortillas. When she began to put on weight, I eased off; pleased to see that something was working while she was still teaching herself. She had to meal plan to stretch what she made—low and behold her father would consume what she created—but at least she isn't underweight anymore.

Don't get me wrong, I was happy with how she looked before too. She's fed now; keeping her belly full is vastly more important than worrying about something as trivial as weight. She could gain an extra hundred and I'd still be in love with her.

My uncle, however, is a fucking pig. He is weary of Nadia, and says she is bad news. He never goes into specifics but I've seen the way he scowls at her despite her manners and respect towards him as an adult and a police officer. The fucker and I have nearly come to blows more than a handful of times because of the way he speaks of her and his glaring lack of respect. Mentioning her father and her mom, how he's abusive, she's a whore, and the way it will turn out the same. I beg to differ, if she becomes like either of them, I know deep in my heart she will see it before it's too late and will change.

Us though? I stuck to her like glue after that fight. There was something about her that held me captive and wouldn't let up. I found myself curiously sneaking glimpses of her in the hallway as she moved between her friends. Always the quieter one of the four, hands and arms wrapped securely around her books as she held them to her chest, and her backpack hanging on one shoulder stuffed full of whatever secrets she kept in there.

Her grey eyes would snap from one face to the next as fellow students filed past her, pretending she was invisible, but as much as she might have been to them, she was increasingly becoming the center of my whole world. By the time I finally grew a pair and asked her out to a football game I had already memorized her routine, making me a certifiable weirdo.

That night, she sat in the front row of the stands, trying to keep up with what was happening on the field and faking her interest. I can still see her, in my mind's eye, following the ball and jumping up to cheer for our team at the wrong times. Poor girl was so embarrassed but I caught her attention and it boosted my confidence. She made me play better, play harder, run faster, all while keeping those beautiful silver eyes focused on me.

Then came the last game of the season. It was out third or fourth down when I finally said to hell with my inhibitions and made my move. Half time hit and I chose to join her instead of my team in the locker room. Wrapped up in a jacket, black beanie that blended with her dark hair, comfortable and warm, she leaned over the rail and smiled at me. She was so fucking stunning and I was already wrapped around each of her fingers. I shoved the toe of my cleats into the fence under the bleachers and pulled myself up. My gloved hands gripped the bar tight when she leaned further over, the tips of her toes barely keeping her grounded when I crushed my lips to hers.

CHAPTER THREE

Today

As soon as I left my mom's I stopped and picked Zap & Wes up from Wes's parents. They have more room there, my poor mom couldn't house Zap with as big as he is, even if she wanted to. Dude is a giant, would have taken both couches and left Wes nowhere to go except the floor.

The sun's still high enough in the sky headlights aren't needed for driving, and considering we are going to a bonfire, everything will be lit up anyhow. When we get to the field several others are already setting up; like ants on a mission, moving around one another with ease and avoiding collisions. Tailgates are down, chairs are pulled out, coolers packed to the top with drinks, I think there is a keg or two around here somewhere, and they definitely didn't forget the beer pong tables. Typical high school slash college kid shit. Speaking of, there are a lot alumni here too; not just me creeping around with my boys.

The captain of the baseball team, from the class ahead of me, is sprawled out on the top of his truck cabin—leaning back on a palm with his letterman on, suck-starting a glass bottle. *Fucking loser*. Who wears their letterman four years after they graduate? Pricks who peaked in high school, that's who.

A few cars down from him is the cheer squad huddling together and giggling at a pair of guys who are more my speed—the outcasts and aggies. I would say cowboys but this isn't the south, we don't have the same climate here for southern influence like they do in say Texas or some shit. Therefore Wranglers, tucked t-shirts, and baseball caps are as good as it gets. I think one or two of them may show goats or something to that effect but that's it, no 'cows' in sight.

Then there's your run-of-the-mill students who don't particularly belong to any group but have built their own little cliques. They come for the beer and the stories to reminisce over later, sitting back and watching everyone like candy-cameras perched on the wall—tailor made for gossip. Back in the day, that was me and my guys, the outcasts. Even though I was on the football team, I didn't spend my time around a bunch of jocks. Why? There's too much testosterone, typically synthetic, and unnecessary ego fights. A lot of the same guys who play also lifted weights and when your state isn't known for its football, you find notoriety elsewhere. Me though? I played my ass off, managed my grades, and had fun. That's all there is to do in here anyway, other than get in trouble and I wasn't quite there yet.

Sliding out of Delinquent, all three of us quickly hunt down a much-needed drink. I opt for soda, the other two snag something mixed they won't remember the name of later—err, they won't remember the night. As we wait for the vibe to pick up, we make our rounds, chatting up some guys we shared a few classes with and the occasional girl. None of which are giving Wes the time of day, he's going to have a long weekend at this rate. Zap, however, keeps looking over his shoulder for someone specific which has me concerned for his tender heart.

Honestly, I don't want to mull around and shoot the shit just to pass the time when I'm fully capable of sitting in the car and people watching. The younger girls always make goo-goo eyes in my direction then attempt to chat me up, ask me questions about where I have been, how school is going, if they can go for a ride in the Civic, and it grates my nerves. They see a face, whether it's pretty or not is debatable, and someone who looks an awful lot like a 'bad boy.' Don't get me wrong, I'm not innocent...at all...but I'm not the type of bad they're hoping for. I'm just a leather jacket wearing, smooth talking, knuckle head who came back from college for one night—one girl.

"Heyyy Kalebbbb." I hear someone croon, and I cringe.

Twisting at the waist, my heart picks up speed when I see Ivy but then it stalls when I notice Nadia isn't with her. It's just the three Stooges she claims as friends. Giving her a tight smile, I lift my cup to say hello and turn back to Wes with a quickness, groaning at the same time.

"Is she coming?"

"Who?" Zap asks.

"That soul sucking harpy, Ivy."

"Oh yeah? She down for sucking my soul out of me?" Wes teases.

"Shut the fuck up, idiota. You know I can't stand her ass."

"Yeah yeah, you put up with her though."

"It's so good to see you, Rey." Ivy purrs as the nightmare appears beside me, hooking her arm into the crook of mine. She beams like a rat that stole the cheese—she doesn't get the courtesy of being the cat, fucking lunatic.

27

"Wish I could say the same, Ivy." I bite back. Ready to chew on my tongue and spit the damn thing out if it keeps me from speaking with her. Matter of fact, I may just gnaw my arm off in the process; get her infuriating touch off of me.

"Oh now come on, that wasn't very convincing." She muses.

"Wasn't meant to be."

Shrugging out of her hold and vacating her proximity, I squeeze myself between Zap and Wes. Zap isn't interested in high school meat, my guy likes the cougars, but he sees something in her—unfortunately not a bullet. This is the only disappointment I reserve for my friend, as he could do much better than Ivy, especially with the older girls. Usually, if she isn't at least ten years older than him, she won't register on his radar. Wes though, he'd fuck a porcupine if you told him which hole to hit.

Ivy huffs and pouts when she can't get to me, crossing her arms over her chest as her bottom lip pokes out—bitch only makes passes at me when Nadia isn't around. I ought to tell her, watch Nadia beat her ass and grin like Cheshire when she cries to me for help. Nadia and I split up when I left for college. She wanted the break more than I did but if she demanded the winning lottery numbers, I would throat-punch someone over their prize-winning ticket.

In the end, I wasn't sure why she needed the space when I thought we were doing so well together. Eventually it clicked, her abandonment issues. She had to control what happened with us or face a harsher ache when she looked in the mirror.

"I'm happy to see you though. You're looking good too. College life is definitely your scene." Ivy adds. Not so subtly reminding me she exists.

For fucks sake, someone come get this girl.

Wes steps in as Oliver and Wren try to redirect Ivy's attention when I don't reply to her. They're picking up what I'm throwing down even if the blind bimbo isn't. Unfortunately, they rather save her feelings than correct her behavior—same can't be said for my friends, I'd drag them over hot coals if needed.

"Iv, let's get a drink." Wren pipes up, Oliver adding to it. "Yeah, maybe we can find some of that trashcan punch you like. I heard Tommy brought some to the last party and he's sitting on his truck right now, he always has the good shit."

"Oh yeah, that sounds great! Rey, do you want anything?" She asks, still vying for my attention. If Nadia knew how shitty her friend is being, let's just say I'd watch that ass chewing before getting her out of here before someone tries to press charges.

"No. Oliver, when's Nadia going to be here?" I ask, seeing Ivy bristle out of the corner of my eye—jealous cunt.

"She went home after the ceremony," he answers with a shrug. "Wanted to get permission from her dad or something like that. You know how she walks on eggshells around him."

Yeah...I do.

"Gotcha, thanks."

Waving them off, I sigh to myself in disappointment. Something tells me Nadia going home wasn't the best thing to do, even if it was the smartest. I hate her dad, to put it lightly. Her friends are a nuisance too, thankfully Nadia isn't very impressionable, but her dad? He sends me into a blinding rage. Out of the few disagreements we've had, they were always about him and how he treats her like dog shit.

I'll bitch about it until I am blue in the face too; she deserves a family that will place her on a damn pedestal, encourage her when she needs it, and love her without any damn conditions. Not one that has her scrubbing the running boards or bleaching the walls, or treating her like a personal slave—Cinderelli, Cinderelli, night and day, oh Cinderelli.

I need to busy myself or I'll end up being pissy all night—ruin her celebration, whenever she gets here.

A loud rumbling growl catches my attention and pulls me away from where I stand scowling between Wes and Zap. A devilish smile creeps across my face, arm hairs standing on end when my eyes land on the Challenger trying to crawl across the grass and park. 'Bitch Maker' is painted across the door skirt in an off white, almost blending in with the remainder of the pearl gloss. Blacked out rims, heavy tint, and the hard thump of bass pulses from the stunning piece of machinery. She's built for the drag but I've had a few runs with her at my side; the sheer power sitting under her hood is what wet dreams are made of. All intake, torque, and raw horsepower.

Reaching the driver side, Sergio Fuentes pops the latch and swings it open with a hushed glide before stepping out. In his typical getup: backwards ball cap, white t-shirt, and dark jeans, he waves inside the cab before the passenger door springs open and a girl climbs out, fixing her skirt, and walks off like it's nothing. Unsurprising, the guy always has girls falling on his dick. He's a player, not that it matters, they like it, he likes it, therefore it works. His circuit and mine rarely cross and even if it did he can have his pick of women with the muscle he drives.

My hand shoots out for a quick bro-shake and slap on the back, greeting one another like we always do. A waft of his over-indulgent cologne smacks me in the face with its overpowering notes with the familiar scent of freshly toked green.

"Fuentes."

"Rey, lookin' good man. How ya been?" He asks, not a bit of Hispanic twang in his accent though he looks more the part than I ever have.

"Not too bad. Didn't expect to see you out this way. You come for the race or do you know someone here?"

"Hmm. You know how I feel about questions, hermano."

Deflection, why am I not surprised?

He runs drugs, I've seen him at a few frat parties making deals as if no one is looking and he has no qualms about getting picked out of a lineup. Pretty sure his side hustle is what pays for his speeding tickets and racing habits. As long as he makes a bill at every gathering, he calls it a win, racing or not.

I've caught wind of him talking to Nadia occasionally, since he graduated after me—it gave him an opportunity. My sources told me she never took the bait and I hope she never does. I rather be the one getting in trouble and tossed into a jail cell, not her, or the both of us together. I have a feeling though, you know the kind that sits low in your stomach and boils until the truth reveals itself? Your 'gut feeling', yeah that's what I have. He's bad fucking news for her, I just can't wrap my head around how or why yet. What's funny is my Uncle thinks I'm the problem when people like Fuentes roam the same streets he patrols.

I'm about to respond to him when he grins and cuts me off. Waving his hand, motioning to the gathering new-grads filling the field, one carful after another.

"Came for the race and a few of the sights. You in your rig today?"

AKA, he came to sell.

"Yeah, parked over there." I point a couple of vehicles down. A few people standing at the hood and taking pictures with their flip phones. Kinda rude to take photos with other people's cars but who am I to complain? As long as they don't touch her, I'm golden.

"Any new work? You know you can't gap me but you're fun to run side to side with. Those last two races put the fear of God in me." The asshole teases me.

"That's because you can't fucking drive. You have all that power and still death grip the wheel instead of letting your machine drive for you. You've got to let go, man. Too much control will have you jerking the wheel and sliding off the pavement."

"Fightin' words, Rey. Fightin' words. Come on, show me what you got. I just put a new system in mine, only a bit of added weight and sound, does nothing for the performance."

"Invest in headphones. Easier on the wallet, still get your music in."

"You got a solution for everything?"

"Sometimes."

We laugh it off then saunter in the direction of the Civic, occasionally stopping to check out another car or truck but not as impressed with what we find. It's not easy for high school kids to get their mitts on the same equipment we install in our cars. Maybe one day they will be in the same races and we can give them some friendly pointers, before the bad ones come in and ruin all the fun—preferring danger and death over the thrill of a ride.

Yeah, I didn't mention that. It's funny—like *Grease* all over again with the Scorpions showing up and turf wars. There's a bad bunch anywhere you go and trust me when I say I've met my own set of rivals. Clayton Summers, Dillon Smith, and Patrick Tomlin are the shits that run rampant through Hazelwood and the surrounding towns.

Most of the time they're sitting at the local diner hazing the patrons but occasionally my uncle runs them off. The only perk of being related to a cop—he helped clean the place up and wards against the riff raff. That was before he left the department and moved to one a few towns over. When I was sixteen he got into a fight with a suspect and was accused of excessive force. Shocker, a hot head strapped with a gun—what could go wrong.

From what my mom has told me, he's calmed down a lot and is doing better but that's not important. What is, is he's on my side when it comes to dealing with Clayton and his goons. Which, I'm sure they will show up at the race this weekend. Thankfully I'll be busy, hopefully too consumed with my alternate plans to play into their foolish games.

On our way in, I squeezed some numbers and crunched the time. If I get Nadia home early enough, I can manage the race tomorrow then have another day or two for my mom and head home Monday. Perhaps I'll finally convince her she needs to run away with me. That's the goal, get the both of us out of here where we can build a life we are proud of rather than one she hides from. I want this with her, to be stupidly wrapped around each other's fingers and so in love it makes you gag.

As soon as Fuentes and I reach the car, I pop the hood and yank it up. The hood struts keep the fiberglass lifted while he looks over the shiny new intake I installed and the cable management courtesy of Zap. There's a whole lot more done to her: ECU tuning, the mounts for the new NOS system, you know...the good stuff.

"Damn bro, she looks good. You've dropped some major cash into her since the last time we chilled. How's she running?"

"Like a fuckin' dream, man. Crisp handling, glides through drifts. Increased the steering sensitivity so she doesn't take a firm hand anymore. Lightened her up a bit when I swapped out the aluminum for fiberglass. Even more when I installed the spoiler. She's so damn light I catch air on a few of the practice tracks."

"Sheeeeeeeeeh. What are her times on an eighth mile?"

"Six point eight."

"Hell yeah, you sure you don't want to put her on a drag? She'd smoke most of the other imports. It would be a hell of a time seeing her put a few of the rice burners to shame."

"Nah man, I don't like those straight shots. It's all about the curves."

He laughs and nods, hands resting near the still-cooling radiator as he leans over and starts doing a visual comparison to Bitch Maker. Truth be told, the only thing that gives him an advantage is his booster. He has too much weight in his car, it could be faster but he likes all of the bells and whistles—anything to get the girl.

Sucked into the conversation, I tune out the rest circling around us. Even Wes and his inevitable hunt for pussy and Zap doing...well, Zap things. Before I know it, the sun has dropped and now hides behind the treetops. Finally realizing Nadia isn't at my side, I look over my shoulder to clock her and my heart sinks.

Where the fuck is she?

I hoped she wouldn't give up this last night out before real adult responsibilities kicked her in the ass, but now I'm not so sure. Knowing her dad he will have chores lined up from here to Memphis by sunrise.

Damn it, I hope I didn't waste an entire weekend coming out here, I mean, there's still the race and my mom but I came for Nadia. Maybe I should have told her I would be here. I missed her birthday and wanted to surprise her by just showing up; now I'm not sure I played those cards right. This was the only way I figured I could make it up to her. Fuck, don't get me started on missing her graduation too—I had a good excuse, I was taking final exams but still I failed her and that does some terrible shit to my head.

Slipping my hand into the front pocket of my jacket, I grip the plastic device in my fist before dragging it out and looking at the screen. It lights up, but there's nothing except the time and cellular coverage staring back at me. No texts, no calls, not even a damn voicemail. What good are these fucking things if the one person you want to hear from doesn't use it?

Shit.

Shit, shit, shit.

"Hey," I call out to Fuentes before stopping myself.

"Yeah? What's up?"

Abandoning my phone, I snag the hood and bring it down in a firm thud, latching it closed with the hood pins piercing both sides.

"Have you seen Nadia tonight?"

"Nadia...? Oh, Pierce? Yeah, she's over there."

I whip around so fast to look where he's pointing, nearly hitting the bumper and tumbling in the process but fuck me there she is.

God I love her.

CHAPTER FOUR

Time stopped about five minutes ago, at least I think it did, hell maybe longer for all I know. I've been consumed tracking every damn move she's made since I laid eyes on her. Music I once could lip sync word for word is now muted by the heavy thump of my heart.

I've waited for this day for weeks, no months, and now that it's here I don't know what the hell to do. Panic, that sounds like the most plausible thing really, just fall the hell over and hide in a shell—a human sized armadillo if you will. After years of knowing this woman, fawning over every fucking thing about her, having memorized her morning routine, to knowing how she prefers her coffee—suddenly I'm a deer in headlights.

The fuck is wrong with me? Love, stupid ass, you're in love with her.

She isn't new, this isn't some newfound crush. We'd simply pick up where we left off if you think about it. As if zero time has passed between her breaking it off with me and today. At least that's how it feels. I've kept myself busy, sliding through life, waiting for this very moment and now my damn feet won't move. Shit, maybe they're buried in the ground and it's the earth refusing to let me join her. Or, perhaps someone wound trailer straps around me when I was too gone to notice, then tied me to the front of the car. Maybe this is a cruel dream and I'm still in my dorm room playing with myself under the blankets.

Whatever it is, goddamn, I need it to let go.

From several yards away I can already feel the soft warmth of her sliding through my calloused grip. The thick, silk-like locks of her hair tangled between my fingers as I knot them in my hand and guide her head back. Then her mouth... fuck. Lush lips, painted with a simple chapstick to keep them from drying too much. Pink, and plump, and mouthwatering.

I'm going to combust right here.

The devil woman herself is decked out in black Converse, denim shorts, and her favorite Mötley Crüe shirt. The same one I've seen her wear for different occasions, even dressed down and curled up in bed. She's worn it so many times the fibers are soft, fragile, and ready to rip with one hard yank. To see her fall out of that damn thing? Heaven. Slight curves, flawless pale skin, the faded summertime freckles sprinkled across her shoulders; she's a dream to watch undress.

Her hair is up today, instead of falling in thick swaths, teasing glimpses of her face. As much as I like when she wears it down, seeing the way it frames every bend and curve of her features, giving me an inhibited view of her neck, kryptonite. I've raked my lips over her pulse as it jumped at the sides until they became raw and the sweet taste of her ingrained itself into my flesh. In the few moments where I lost all decency, I sank my teeth into her until she whined under me and turned different shades of red.

The style makes her look more her age versus how put together she looks when it's down; waved to perfection and so shiny it looks like a halo at times—something I could thank Ivy for I suppose. This is the only time

I will ever give Ivy a compliment, so take it and run. Nadia appears less burdened this way; the tendrils of pain and hurt haven't dragged her into the terrors yet. She's a warrior in her own rite and she owns it.

Dumbfounded with the ground anchoring me in place, I lean against the front of the Civic and just watch. The fiberglass is cooler after being parked for an hour or so, I think, but the random soft tinks and clinks still ring under the car's hood every once in a while. Easy to miss if you were wrapped up in the vibe beginning to pick up at this bonfire. Loud music, rambunctious talking, and the soft crackle of flames catching on old skids and branches someone gathered for this night alone.

I'm ready to sweep her off her feet, no joke. Should I be chivalrous about it, hold her up bridle style where I can look down into those chilly eyes before I devour her pillowy lips? Or I could, you know, throw her over my shoulder. Allow my roughened hands to knead her thighs and ass as I walk off into the woods with her. True caveman shit—I mean, I'm feral for her as much as I am obsessed, being a barbarian wouldn't be too far off the reservation.

I can't decide. Really. There's only one way I can caveman myself into her life again and I want to make sure I do it the right way, that she can't find the strength in herself to get rid of me again. That we are now, we are forever, and she wouldn't dream of letting me go. Fuck, I'm disgusting. Daydreaming about both demolishing her and praising her violently.

Watching Nadia could be a new favorite pastime; high-definition visual of a walking wet dream. If there were a way for me to have tabs on her at all times, I'd make it happen. If she denies me, refuses to run away from here, and tie herself to me, I'd still creep on her. She wouldn't be safe in that sense, my lurking eyes glued to the woman who's laid silent claim to my very existence.

I'll make my way over to her eventually, once I grow a pair of balls, but where I'm at right now? Observing her curvy frame hoist on the dropped tailgate of her truck, seeing her smile and toss her head back in laughter is becoming a highlight of my fucking night. Frankly, I don't want to intrude or interrupt anything obviously bringing her joy. That's until her sharp, silver gaze performs a head-to-head collision with mine and my world stops.

"Rey, yo man, this party is dank. Let's get out of here." Wes whines at my left. Nearly distracting me from the sight standing a couple yards away—nearly. Unsuccessful at best.

"Get turned down by every prospect so far?" Zap teases, Wes flying off the handle like he always does. And now they have my attention, pulling my focus from Nadia. Five seconds, can't they get along for five damn seconds? I don't want to deal with them, maybe if I ignore them they will go away.

"Man, fuck you. I'm putting itching powder on the couch when we get back to the house."

"Itching powder? You twelve again? Rey, don't pay him any mind. It's a decent party, besides, we came for two reasons and one is staring you down. You going to do anything about that, or just let it simmer?"

"Hmm?" Trying damn hard to tune the two knuckleheads out and hold Nadia's frigid gaze. I fear she's doing a better job at ignoring Oliver who's chattering away next to her and sipping from his red cup.

"Leave him be, Zap. He's a goner. Princess at twelve o'clock."

Nadia eases off the tailgate, finally breaking eye contact, then lifts and slams it shut. It's her dad's beat up piece of junk, but she sees freedom in it. I understand what it means to her, my first car had me running the roads. Let's not forget about the pride I had earning and owning something of my own after hard work. Broke my heart when I traded in my old car for the new one, but things had to be done.

I'm about to push away from the Civic and go to her when Wes pops off and gets into another argument with Zap.

"Would you two knock it the fuck off already? Wes, I swear. You must be on your period or something, acting like a temperamental bitch. You've been going all damn day. Give it a break."

Wes bristles next to me but I don't care. He's quickly ruining all of the good vibes we've hunted for since leaving campus. There's no telling what his problem is, maybe those few months in county lockup have institutionalized him a bit and he's itching to get back to the structure he doesn't have out here.

Go into the military then, fucking titty baby, save us the headache of dealing with the tantrums. Somewhere along the line, his emotional maturity has evaporated and we're the ones dealing with the fallout.

Music picks up around us, two cars finally tuning into the same radio station for surround sound when I realize Nadia's heading my way. My nerves immediately went out the window, subconsciously forcing me to shove my trembling hands into my jacket pockets. Curiosity is holding her attention hostage when she glosses over the car, lingering on the finer details I've spent precious time on. Then, like the calming heat of a cup of hot cocoa, she graces me with a voice that's corrupted every nook and cranny of my thoughts.

"Hey Rey."

Play it cool, stupid.

"Nadi, how've you been?" Damnit she's beautiful.

"Not too bad, I guess."

Not very convincing, Diabolica.

Her eyes are a bit darker under her bottom lashes. I can't help but assess her a bit longer, putting together a mental bullet list of what now haunts her before acting like some Danny Zuko knock off. Shrugging my shoulders solely to shift my jacket around. Too cool to care much—dumb as a box of rocks.

"That's good. Happy graduation day, by the way." Let's mask this with a smirk, maybe that will make it better—blue steel style. Kidding, fuck I'm kidding. Ignore me, I don't know how to be casual.

"Thanks, this your new car?"

Fucking-A, safe territory.

Standing up from the hood, we both stare down at the other woman in my life—Delinquent. I like how Nadia notices her, notices things about me that tells people she pays attention to what matters to others. Not sure if she knows it, but her awareness means so much. She has a good eye for the little things too. So, every time I fuck up as her husband, she's going to clock it from ten miles away. Lord I hope so, that's a leash I'll gladly let her yank.

"Yeah, want to take a look at her? I've had her for about six months." I start, stepping back to let her have more space to explore my baby.

"Trying to work enough to save up for body modifications, maybe a new intake." I say as I pop the hood for her this time. When in doubt, which I'm swimming in, distract your prey. Pointing to a few things underneath the shell, I explain more of the changes I want to make all while she follows along curiously.

Yep, I bought a new intake not too long ago but she doesn't know that, this is just a shit ton of small talk. Anything to keep her speaking and move the attention off of me onto something else. The car I named after her? Perfect specimen. Teasing my hand over the driver side fender, I can't help the way I look at it. She's buttery in my hands, easy to control. There's no way about it, if I move her to the left she eases that way as if there's no such thing as gravity, same with the right. She starts up quietly with a few button presses, then if I treat her just right she wins. I'm only a driver, this car? She's the athlete.

"You're speaking a different language. I don't know a damn thing about cars, Rey. Dumb it down for me."

Heh, anytime Diabolica. I'll teach you whatever you want to know.

Chuckling, a few steps and I'm at her side. Feeling the weight of her very existence next to me, then I guide her back a few inches to protect her delicate fingers from getting caught by the hood when I shut it with a chest punching thud. Leaning again, my ankles and arms crossing, I take Nadia in. All of her. Every. Fucking. Inch.

Her height, the bounce of her hair, the way she keeps her lips slightly parted between speaking. I'm not worthy of it but I could stare at her forever. She's waiting expectantly for me and that fills me with a hunger I've forced myself to avoid for years.

"You wound me, Nadi. I thought you would have learned a bit more in my years away, so you'd actually have something to impress me with."

The second a flash of pain shoots across her face, my stomach drops. Okay, okay, it was a little harsh but we've never coddled one another. Since day one she's dished me a verbal beating I would crawl through hot coals for—some sort of masochist I am. Right as I'm about to word vomit and apologize for being a cocksucker, she hits me with her deliciously-smart mouth.

"And impressing you is important, why?"

Tou-fucking-che.

Alright, smart ass, let's have at it.

Shrugging, I stand tall. Letting her sass roll off me like water and duck feathers—however that saying goes. I'd have her no other way. Grass shifts under my boots as I move around the front of the car and ease my way to the passenger door. Squeezing the handle, it pops open with a noise that's almost deafening to me but no one else seems to notice. This is what she does to me, makes me hyper-vigilant. I zero in on the smallest details and over exaggerate the ones that mean the least.

Opening the door for her without saying a damn thing, I stand back like the gentleman my mom raised me to be, and wait for her to slide inside. As much as she loves silence, the quiet between us isn't comfortable in the least, mostly her though. It makes her fidget and uneasy. Truth be told, I like it when she's a little uncomfortable. She does the craziest shit—one of the entertaining highlights of our nights together.

Jerking my head slightly, motioning her to get in, I make a final pass over the field to see who's not aware of their surroundings and those who should mind their damn business. This is my night, ours if you want to get technical, and the rumors of a new graduate class will not bode any of them well. Best they keep their mouths shut and their heads down.

Nadia sweeps past me and her body spray hits my nostrils with the force of the Juggernauts sledgehammer; ache shooting from my heart all the way to the fucker in my pants. Sinking my teeth into my bottom lip, I fight to stifle the groan she drags out of me.

Jesus H. Christ, save me now.

CHAPTER FIVE

I almost pull a *Dukes of Hazard* by taking a running slide across the car's hood; solely to get in the driver seat quicker but I'm maintaining what fraction of composure I have. I can't help it. There's a new sort of energy rolling through me like a tsunami, crashing with waves so immense they're obliterating that vast majority of my common sense. Giddy over the girl of my dreams sitting in my car, fastening her seat belt like we've done this a million times.

We will...a million and one if that's what it takes.

Folding into my seat, the door latches securely after me; auto-engaging with a dull snap—a mod I made for my dumbass friends. If the worst happens, if I roll this bitch with them in here, the last thing I have to be concerned about is a door popping open and one of them being ejected. Wes says it's morbid to think that way, Zap has my back though. He knows, even in the thick of it, it's safer for all of us to remain locked inside than hitting the unforgiving ground at a hundred-something miles an hour.

Nadia's in my peripherals, familiarizing herself with the inside. Her inquisitive gaze snaps from one feature to the next: dash, center console, gear shift, then she catches the additional gauges attached to my side of the cab. My lips part ready to explain, share a bit more of my favorite distraction, but she turns away.

She looks unsure of herself, those pretty brows pinching together as her hands drop to the harness-belt, nearly white knuckling the black polyester as if it's a lifeline. She must catch me looking since she moves them to the door instead of the restraint, gripping it just as hard as she was clinging to the belt.

Is she scared? Does she think I'll put her in harm's way? Okay, I might, but I'll keep her safe. I know what I'm doing. I've been behind the wheel for years now, hell pit maneuvers are my thing. I've been practicing them on and off a controlled track since I left for school. Not that I'd ever perform one without her knowledge first—and the chance to get out and watch from a safer position. I never want to make her uncomfortable with the things I do on the road. Truthfully, hope boils low in my gut that she will love this—riding with me—as much as I love her being here. I mean, this used to be a bonding moment for us, surely that hasn't changed between then and now.

She'd curl up under the hood and on the frame of my old car, shoes pressed against the grimy coated motor and watch as I broke things apart. I remember the hundreds of questions she used to ask. Sometimes I think she would do it to keep the conversation going, especially on the days where her dad was being a dick— when the silence was pulling her apart. Then other times, I wholeheartedly believe it's genuine curiosity. That, or she just loved looking at me covered in grease; yeah, we'll go with that one.

Fuck me, I want those moments back.

I'm going to take her on one hell of a ride tonight, drive her right down memory-fucking-lane. Late nights, long rides, and relief. I could tell her right now, let her know all the shit that's been swimming in my head for years but how the hell do I even begin explaining it? Giving purpose and story to my words is a bit easier said than done. I've always been better with my hands. Winning Nadia over with some Shakespearean type shit just isn't me, isn't us. Either way, she will go through a thousand emotions and sensations before the night is through—promise.

Hang in there, Diabolica. Tonight's going to be one to remember.

Stabbing the key into the ignition, I flick the power relay switch with a snappy-click then jab the starter with my roughened fingertip. Turning the key the Civic purrs to life and seals away all of my worries and doubts. Unsure if she notices, but I practically melt into the leather of my seat. Every muscle relaxes under the pull of gravity and the anticipation of being in her presence. Finally...finally I'm sharing this with Nadia. Gifting the pieces of myself life stole from her, ones that have felt deprived and starved for longer than I care to admit.

Snagging the stereo dial, the music climbs louder as I twist it to the right, helping drown out the remaining silence tickling the space with electricity. She came here to visit with her friends and I'm practically kidnapping her—finders keepers, fuckers. At minimum I want to make sure she's comfortable, especially with how tense she looked when she first latched her seatbelt.

I'm the better company anyway.

Time to get lost, in her, in the road, in anything except responsibilities and wishful thinking. Away from people who use her because they're too fucking scared to take care of their own shit and need someone else to fight their battles for them. Anywhere but this field with fake friends, jocks that peaked in high school, and the promise of bad decisions.

Back in drive, we creep across the uneven ground, dips and bumps making our departure awkward compared to the lifted trucks and SUV's parked nearby. Fine blades of grass brush along the underside of my car, cleaning away the debris and buffing out of the blemishes, if not there then definitely the backside of my wheels. I don't typically like keeping my vehicle this low to the ground but when you're racing, aerodynamics are important.

Nadia's friends watch as we crawl by them, snagging glances from a few others, and the grins from my boys. They may lack emotional intelligence but they hope I get everything I've yearned for since starting school, and then some.

When the rubber meets the road, all four tires ease into more solid ground, I open her up. Pressing on the accelerator until the needle on my gages jump high and RPM's rocket halfway to the red. Pressing the clutch, my hand grabbing the gear shift, I shift her into second and repeat the motions—launching Nadia back in her seat with every burst of horsepower.

Hearing her breath catch has me fighting a smirk as my hands move easily with the twisting and turning steering wheel. Letting the car practically drive itself while the tires grip the black top—sticky from today's travels.

"How has college been?" She asks, silver eyes focused on the windshield. The words rushed, almost tripped over at the end.

What do I say? That it's a placeholder for the life I really want to have? That I fall asleep with a book on my chest in my dorm instead of her? Or how my classes blend together and I don't remember what I'm doing until the professor re-explains the homework and I just happen to finish it in class? There is so much, but also so little, going on with school.

"Meh, not bad. Keeping my grades up isn't that hard. I work most of the time so I've stayed out of the spotlight. The guys though? Different story. Logan already has a kid and Wes just got out of county."

Clenching the gearshift, I filter through the second-nature movements and push the RPM's higher.

Logan keeps his kid under wraps, not because he's ashamed, but his relationship is rocky and it hurts him half the time. She's vindictive and he loves her—I can't fault him for that. He's trying though, to let her go and move on, poor fucker has his eyes set on the wrong rebound and he knows it. I've warned him and if he doesn't want to hear it, then that's on him; I'm too wrapped around this tornado's finger to keep leading that horse to water. While I don't speak about his dealings, or Wes's, Nadia is safe, I know I can talk to her about anything even the bad shit when it goes down.

"That doesn't sound terrible. Say, if you could give me any advice when it comes to school, or getting out of Hazelwood, what would it be?" She huffs through the pressure on her body from the harness; looking at me now instead of the scenery as it whips by.

Now we're talking. Run away with me, that's all you have to do. We won't have anything but each other at first but I promise I'll make sure you're happy.

"Honestly, I wouldn't waste your time with school until you know what you want to do. There are so many different avenues and jobs out there that don't require a college degree, and they pay just as much, if not more, than those do."

She snaps at me, in her charming way. "Ahhh, that's helpful, I guess. Not really."

Chuckling at half mast, I shrug. I don't want to talk about school. I understand that's her focus but damn, she just graduated. Take a night off, workhorse. Relaxed, my body twists a fraction to the side. Left hand resting on the steering wheel where I could see more of her and she could look at me all she pleases. She always did stare.

"Always such a curt smartass, Nadi. The things I could do to that mouth of yours now that you're a big girl."

Devilish joy fills me when her face reddens. She surprises me, responding that way. We've been too close for too long for her to be bashful or shy. While I may not be a capitalist like Wes, I'm going to take a very small page out of his book and have that same look on her beautiful face all night.

"Thank you, though. For telling...sharing. I don't have the patience to waste my time so I'll have to keep your words of wisdom in mind."

"See that you do. College is unnecessarily expensive. Especially when you can do something else. Something good."

The road finally comes to an end, trees framing both sides while a more open space sits ahead of us, beyond a blinking yellow light. If we go left we'll circle back around, hug the mountains and take hours to return. Have a night where it's just us, slow driving, low music, and all vibes.

Or we can go right and head into the city—Detroit is unpredictable in the summer. An evening of high octane, steamy windows, and street races. The kind that leaves you on the edge of your seat. The kind people search for and never taste again.

"Yeah. What makes you think I want to do anything good, Rey?"

"You planning on committing murder or something?" I tease.

"Nah, not yet."

And like that, I turn the steering wheel to the right and gun it.

Game on.

On the highway, with the windows down and air flooding the cabin, Nadia reaches over and wrenches the volume knob to the right, sending *Tesla* blaring around us. At least she hasn't forgotten I'm a music guy, the oldies of course. None of this new age bullshit where you can't understand a fucking thing they're saying or lacks story to the lyrics. Pink Floyd, Cinderella, Foreigner, Bad Company; you know, the good shit.

This is exactly how I lose myself—by finding comfort in how easy the Civic glides through traffic with my girl at my side.

From the corner of my eye, I see her reach up and gather her hair, pulling it down to the side of her neck. She pins it there, preventing it from flailing all over the place—taming the dark cloud of soft strands, inadvertently rewarding me with a better view of her profile. The rough air has captured her body wash, perfume, what the hell ever, long ago. I hope to God it clings to the leather interior so I can have a part of her with me when I'm forced to let her go at the end of the night. It will have to tide me over until I get her back in the car after the weekend.

Reclined in my seat, one arm reached out at the steering wheel's ten-o-clock, the other resting at four, we skate around the ass of a tractor-trailer when I get a wild hair. Every time I turn or maneuver sharply, she lets out a little gasp. Pressing abruptly on the accelerator, she jolts in her seat and sucks in a breath when her head moves in a forced nod. She snaps her sassy mug my way when I chuckle. Tilting my head, I can't help but grin at her; a canine snagging the cushion of my bottom lip. She glares a bit longer then turns to the side, staring back out the window as the suburbs zip past us in a blur.

The sun is far beyond the mountains, leaving a warm glow behind them as we approach the city. The skyline is already lit up, painted in a sharp blue from the Renaissance Center; it's cold and abrasive neon clashing with the other buildings but still stands out against the darkened sky on the eastern side. A rainbow of red, gold, and green light does its best to outshine the corruption and poverty running rampant on the city streets. A mask like no other, from afar there's glitz and glamor, billions of dollars' worth of money but under it all the city is rotten. Still, the lights are stunning.

I have driven this route hundreds of times, and I'm still left speechless on every drive in. Nearly every one of my runs has been at night too, that way I get to witness the splendid lie that is Detroit. Another concrete covered Wild West with gang violence in the projects, highways littered with trash and debris, and alley ways that have seen just as much bloodshed as garbage pickups.

Under the same lights though? Families are born, lives are changed, and love is found in the most unlikely of places. Fitting as the love of my life is suddenly shifting in her seat next to me, tucking her legs under her; making herself small in a world where she already feels tiny.

Joke's on you, Diabolica, you're the center of mine and that makes you immeasurable.

We're almost to the off ramps leading into shopping districts when the low hum of a bike overtakes the purr of the car. Checking my side mirrors first, then the rear view, I hunt down the source. Sports bikes, this I know, I can tell by the absence of the deep rumble baggers have. Which means the Blacktop Butchers are not casing us.

Sitting up in my seat, I reach over, putting my hand on the shoulder of Nadia's seat, holding the steering wheel steady when I check the blind-spots. Sure enough, there's five of them. Staggered in a pyramid style placement, one leading point in a blacked-out get-up. Original. I can't say shit, Delinquent is blacked out too. Criminals have that about them, make it black and make it scary—oogly boogly.

The leading bike moved up beside Nadia's window, running dangerously close to the car, and knocked a gloved knuckle on the glass moving at eighty down the highway. As self-aware as she is, she clocked them just as quickly as I did—now holding a stare with the biker.

Lord help me, don't let her fall for two wheels instead.

He waves playfully at her, tilting his head towards the off ramp coming up; telling me to pull over. I'm about to hit my blinker and move over, when Nadia lifts her hand and flips him off. The rider outside of her window is shaking his head now, jolting enough to look like he's laughing. That's when I see the phantom black 'E' sticker on his visor. Flicking the indicator up, the clicking sound barely snaps over the thumping music and 1,000cc engines. Tonight's about to take another fun turn. If I know anything about this fucker, shit's about to go down.

"You wanna get in trouble?"

Nadia jumps, whipping around to look at me and my heart fucking stops—breathe Kaleb.

CHAPTER SIX

"W hat?" she asks.

"Do you wanna get in trouble? With me?"

"What the fuck is that supposed to mean? I thought we were just going for a ride."

Let me introduce to you the man you've been missing, Nadia.

Giving her a side glance, my right hand lowers to the shifter, dropping a gear as I let off the gas pedal. The RPM's skyrocket into the red, making the exhaust clap loud, and the engine groan under the forced deceleration. She's still looking at me, even as the group of bikes split, one on both sides, one leading, and two following now. We all ease across three lanes, rubber gripping the different levels of uneven pavement before meeting the off ramp.

Nadia turns and looks through the back and out the window, her harness keeping her secure in the seat, making her strain to rubberneck at our tail. We roll over a small bump that jolts her at the end of the ramp, a stop light looming ahead of us and bathing the street in its haunting glow. I know exactly where we are, I won't need an escort but this is their territory with rules to follow.

"Who the fuck are these guys? Rey..."

"Ellum Syndicate, sweetheart. Hang on."

"What are they doing? Do you know them? Where are we going?"

"Nadia, sit down. I'll answer your questions in a moment, let me drive."

Heat blasts across my face when she practically explodes next to me. I know she hates being told what to do but I need to focus—not because I'm intimidated but because I need to be safe on these torn up roads, especially with the riders around me. It could go from a simple convoy to thrown rocks, downed bikes, and pissed off riders throwing fists. She can wait, hell she can sit there quietly and use those pretty peepers of hers to figure out what's going on too.

Sure enough, they weave around potholes and stand up on their pegs as we hit dips and bumps. You know, for the influx of money they have coming through the syndicate you'd think they would move somewhere that's a bit friendlier on their equipment. The fuck are they supposed to do if the cops show up and raid their joint? All the pigs would need to do is throw down road spikes and they're all going to jail with a rap sheet longer than a CVS receipt.

We're on the edge of the projects, dilapidated homes sit on both sides of the road, windows boarded up from either raids or kids just being kids. Multiple vehicles of all varying shapes and sizes remain parked in front yards, chain link fences, stocky dogs that spend more time barking at kids on bicycles and the occasional homeless person shoving their cart down the sidewalk than sleeping or eating their high protein diets fit for kings.

Further through the neighborhood, the houses fade out and give way to something more industrial. Old brick buildings start to appear with scaffolding still attached to the sides where the city attempted to remodel them into luxury condos. Too bad they lost the community upkeep bid and had to abandon them. Power lines crisscross over the road and from one property to another, the transformers barely hang on to wooden pillars that used to carry more power than many of the skyscrapers downtown.

On the far end, sitting on the left, is a newer warehouse encased in metal with glass windows painted black on the interior and exterior. How do I know they're double coated? Because I've been inside, around monsters who walk the world and try to give name to their violent cause. The very vultures who feed people in the neighborhood while simultaneously extorting them for money and protection. It's all for show, the main objective is to keep the rival gangs out of the area and maintain the cleanliness of the streets yet paint them in blood and body parts. I never should have come here in the past, but I did and now when they command you, you follow.

Easing the Civic into their rough driveway, the bikes flank all sides of the car like they did on the highway. The riders hit their kill switches almost in unison, plunging each bike into silence outside of the soft tinks from their heated engines. I power off the car too, the music dying when the electricity does and all I can hear now is how hard Nadia is breathing.

She's scared. I know I said that I'd never put her in harm's way, and I meant that, but sometimes you speak terrible shit into existence without meaning to. So, here we are.

"When we get out, don't say anything. If something looks sketchy, look away, don't ask questions, and only engage in polite conversation. A lot of these guys are on power trips and you're pretty, they will try to hit on you to undermine me but as long as we don't respond we'll be okay." I try to coach her, knowing she's barely listening to me and looking for an escape rather than survival tactics.

"Nadia, now's the time to tell me you understand. I need that from you, please."

"I..." she begins but stalls when people approach the car. "I understand."

Calmly, I lean over and unlatch her harness. Drawing the straps off of her shoulders and away from her lap, trying to be a gentleman amidst the chaos, but truth be told I'm terrified. I have no doubt this impromptu visit will end without commotion but I know how to exist here–she doesn't.

She's breathing too fast, if she doesn't relax then she is going to start hyperventilating and pass out. Unbuckling my harness, I reach over and cup her face. Making contact with her unnaturally silver eyes, running both thumbs over her cheeks to keep her attention on me; guys gathering at the front passenger wheel waiting for us to exit.

"Easy sweetheart, slow deep breaths for me. I won't let anything happen to you, okay? We will hang out here for a little while, see what Emmett wants, then we'll leave—get back to our drive."

"You promise?"

"Promise. I'll come around and open the door for you. Keep it locked until I'm there."

"O—okay."

Releasing her, I climb out and slap hands with a few of the guys. They yank me in for a hug and clap their hands on my upper back but I'm not focused on them. I need to get to the passenger side and let her out so people aren't staring at her through the glass like she's in the aquarium and waiting for a shark to come gobble her up.

"Rey! My man."

Hearing that familiar croon, I twist and nod at the six-foot-five sore thumb of a man who runs this Ellum faction. The Ellum originated in Philly and has since moved across the northern United States. It's run by men between twenty-five and forty because the other g's end up in jail or a hole in the ground. He took over about two years ago, right around the time I met him at a club with Wes on one of his many girl-hunts. We got tore the fuck up—I barely remember half the night but we come to hang out from time to time, which I have learned is more than I ever wanted.

Emmett Carver—mogul son—heir to an empire he wants to dismantle and throw into the lake. Dark hair, dark eyes, built like 2001's Vin Diesel. His parents dote and throw money at him but the fucker is out here slinging bullets, drugs, and running the second most prolific biker gang in Detroit. Right after the Blacktop Butchers—different scene though. The way he is with his little sister, and baby brothers though? You'd never think they were family nor that he was a gang leader.

Stepping away from his boys, I reach my hand out and shake him with a firm grip. He yanks me in with a slap on my back like they did. Releasing my hand, he cradles the back of my head—hugging me like some old man who hasn't seen his son since war.

"Yo Em."

"It's good to see you, Fam. The fuck you been hiding?"

"School, man. Keeping those grades up, holding down my gig. Need the cash to throw into the car." I answer.

He releases me, both of his hands now finding my biceps with a firm grip. He looks at me from head to toe and back up—sizing me to see if I still fit into the realm of what he's looking to recruit. Sucks for him, I won't be persuaded that easily. He could throw a stack on my lap tomorrow and try to buy me, promise to deck out Delinquent and have me on the track in the blink of an eye but no. I want to do this my way, it's my life and my future on the line, I'm not going to let the promise of ease and money and fame steer me away.

"Speaking of your Matchbox car, I see you got a girl with you today. You going to leave her there, in this heat, use her as an excuse to leave early? You know how I feel about people who show up for the food, then run."

"And let her sit there and look pretty behind glass? Not a chance. On my way to help her out."

"Such a gentleman, don't let me keep you. Go on, get your girl."

Your girl. Yeah, mine.

Wrong place and wrong fucking time, Kaleb. Get Nadia and get this shit over with, the riders wouldn't have pulled us this way if they didn't want us here. Rounding the front of the car, I reach her door and hear the locks disengage when I grab the handle. Popping it free, she twists in her seat. Converse meeting dirt at her exit, she clears the open door and instantly takes hold of my hand, wrapping one around it as the other laces our fingers together—my heart leaps into my throat.

Fuck me.

Em joins us a few seconds later, his inquisitive gaze sliding across Nadia a little too long before a playful smirk pulls at his mouth.

"Emmett Carver. Sorry, I didn't catch your name." He introduces himself, attempting to be a charming devil, extending his hand for her to shake.

"I didn't give it." She bites back, tone even and dry. Nadia didn't look away or back down. Shifting slightly, I focus on her, seeing how she's going to handle the situation and if I'll have to fight my way out of this or if

Em will accept her smart mouth as a greeting. To my relief, he laughs and pushes his hand forward a bit more, shoulders relaxing, his stance shifting into more of an unintimidating lean that you see between friends.

"Nice to meet you, Smartass. Go on, shake it, let's see if that attitude matches your grip."

Nadia doesn't hesitate, she lets go and slaps her hand in his where he feigns the power of her strength when she squeezes his palm. He grabs his shoulder and hollers, hissing when his boys rush up thinking she's doing real damage but he waves them off; delicately shaking her hand after his dramatics. Em claps his free one on the back of hers and brings it up, kissing the faint scars on her knuckles. A wave of jealousy rushes through me, settling in my jaw between my gritted teeth—dickhead.

"Alright, death grip, what's your name?"

"Nadia."

"Pretty. You Rey's girl? Or you here to shop? I'm sure any of my boys would love to have a cute thing like you hanging on their arm."

"If I was in the market for a fast track to the penitentiary, sure."

A few lurkers hanging behind Em crack up at that, the sounds of their varying laughs mix with their clapping hands and hooting. Em doesn't say anything for a moment. You can see the wave of intrigue and a slight bit of annoyance pass over his features but he schools them and smiles at her. His tongue moves in his mouth like he's tasting something he has to swallow a few times to get down—pride.

"That's enough, Nadia." I chime in. Em snaps his gaze to mine and the mask comes down, covering the violence behind it.

"Come in, we're about to throw some food on the grill. Celebration, successful run and because we fucking can. Nadia, join us, please. Let me introduce you to some of the other girls and show you that we're just a big ass chosen-family here."

"She won't be leaving my side." My tone is uncompromising and color me fucking grateful she doesn't say anything as I speak boldly for her. She can rip me for it later, right now we have an appearance to make.

"Fine, fine, food and good vibes it is!" He relents, both hands lifting in that all too familiar hands up-don't shoot pose, smirking at my girl. Cocky asshole. I hope his siblings don't turn out like him, one Em is enough on this fucking rock. Reluctantly, we follow him; flanked by riders who are reaching for women as we move across the drive to the open garage-style door. Grills are lined up on both sides, billowing heat, buffet style and my damn stomach growls when the scent of charred meat hits my nose.

Nadia quietly looks around, taking inventory of our surroundings for reasons I hate as we move deeper inside. Four feet in front of the grills are folding tables loaded with fixings: tomatoes, lettuce, condiments, cheese, chips, grilled corn, tortillas, plates & napkins too. Beneath them, coolers loaded with ice and drinks so high they remain propped open. To the untrained eye, this looks like a normal gathering of families but I know better.

"Rey—" Nadia whispers at my side. Pulling my attention away from the set up my gaze follows her eyesight to several more people huddled around another table. As if they knew she was watching, they leaned over with fingers pressed to their noses, sweeping across the metal finish. I know exactly what the hell they're doing, which they confirm as they stand straight and start sniffing hard. Nadia is tense at my side, probably the first time she's ever seen someone snort a line of blow.

"Don't look at them. Come on, let's sit." Urging her away, we manage to find a single seat available on a couch that has seen better days. The faux leather is cracking with peekaboos of fabric beneath, some of the damage has been patched but not successfully. Not to mention the cat scratches on the arm rests, and gnaw marks on the feet where dogs spend too much time being bored rather than useful.

Squeezing between two people, I drag Nadia onto my lap. This might have not been the plan, bringing her into the den, but we will make do. She doesn't fight me, thankfully. My hands find her hip and thigh almost immediately when someone begins to pass out plated hamburger patties and hot dogs. I rather she didn't eat here, if she's hungry we can go somewhere else; to my relief she declines and relaxes back into me as much as she can. Her back pressing against my chest, trying to look like she might belong here, even if it's only for a moment. Leaning in, my nose grazes the side of her neck before I speak only where she can hear.

"Sorry, I'll get us out of here as soon as I can. Em must want me for something or the riders wouldn't have escorted us in."

"Whatever," she clips quickly.

Yeah, sassy pants. I know that tone.

"Rey, we need to talk." Em states on cue, finding his place on the coffee table before us, too damn close to Nadia. There are paper plates with food littering the top, beer cans, cups of alcohol, and soda. I have a feeling he's trying to intimidate her, ugly for him, he's barked up the wrong damn tree.

"I thought you might, what you got?"

"Your sister's boy."

"Yeah, what about him?"

"He's made waves—a name for himself here. Thought I would give you a heads-up, hopefully talk her out of having anything to do with him because I need him to focus. He gets lost in his phone and fucks up my shipments instead of doing what the hell I pay him to do."

Em leans forward, digging his elbows into the tops of his denim-clad knees while he stares at Nadia. She gives nothing away, even her body language screams 'nice try' all while one of my hands kneads her thigh. I know what the hell he's doing, he's trying to scare her off—making her think I also work for him or will, and that her presence isn't welcome. He failed with my sister, surely he doesn't think he will win with Nadia, her attitude and backbone is far sharper.

"I don't know what you want me to do. He's a grown man and though she's only seventeen, I can't tell her to do shit."

"That's where you're wrong. She can kick rocks or he can go away for a long time. I'm trying to keep my operations open and moving in the right direction and she's fucking it up."

"Don't put this on my sister."

"Pussy is dangerous. You should heed the same warning."

"Or you can mind your business." Nadia sneers.

"Watch it, princess. I'll wipe the floor with you before Rey can get his pretty ass off the couch."

"Is this how you speak to all the guests you coerce into your cookouts? You're not much of a host."

"Brave mouth on you—and you..." he looks over at me. "You should control your girl better. I'll let this incident slide once but after that you're going to eat gravel."

"Rey, can we go? Looks like respect isn't a two-way street here." She goes to rise and I yank her down to me.

"We're not leaving yet." She's about to explode when I move the conversation back to the topic at hand. "I'll talk to Ximena but there's no promises, Em. I can only do so much. That's something you might want to take up with him because I've tried to get her to dump his ass for a year now."

"That's not good enough, Rey. You know I expect things to be taken care of a certain way and you're the man that can do it. I better see their relationship disappear before he gets hurt."

"Hurt him then. I don't like his ass to begin with."

Em stalls, sitting up straight. His posture screaming violence, fingers cracking his knuckles trying to rein himself in, eyes dilating like those of a predator. He's ready to strike but Nadia is in the way and he won't hurt her.

There's a long pause in the air, noise dying down momentarily. Several pairs of eyes shift our way, some hesitant to be nosey, others ready to take count of everything as it unfolds. This is what he hates, questioning and denying the things he wants done—immediately, might I add. If he wants to control the world, perhaps he should cozy up to his dad and go the white-collar route instead of the gangster one because there will always be someone who will challenge him.

Em glances to his left, nodding at his right-hand man before he stands. Leaving Nadia's head right at his waist height—putting her in an uncomfortable position that pisses me the hell off.

"I have a job for you."

"No, thanks."

"It wasn't a fucking request, Rey. Wheels moving in ten minutes. Let's go."

CHAPTER SEVEN

This is going so fucking well—not.

I'm practically pushing Nadia off my lap when I call after Em, his stride's unhurried but longer compared to my own. True to my word, she doesn't leave my side while I drag her along with me, catching up with Em at the door to the living area of the warehouse.

Cold air steals the wind from both of our lungs when he rips the door open and cooler air meets us. Ushering us through, it slams behind us, drawing attention from more people within. I swear, everywhere I look there's ten more faces I've never seen before—it's unsettling being the center of attention, when it's gang affiliated.

"Glad you had a change of heart. Go sit at the table."

He heads off, leaving Nadia alone again. She's tense beside me, her palms sweating against mine when we shuffle together. Nodding to an empty seat, I wait for her to sit down before saying anything; I know she's upset with me and has every right to be but being pissed off isn't going to get us out of this any faster.

"I'll be right over there. Remember when I said not to talk to anyone? This would be the best time for you to pretend like you're invisible."

"When we get the hell out of here, you're taking me straight back to the bonfire. I didn't ask for this shit, Rey."

"I know, I know. I'm sorry. I'll take you wherever you want to go as soon as I can. Just...let me take care of things, okay?"

She drops onto a seat and crosses her arms without saying another word. There's no one else to blame except me—had I never come here to begin with, I never would have made it onto Em's radar. It's my own damn fault and I'm going to beat myself up over it while I'm sitting in this painful meeting I want zero part of.

Aching to reach for her, feel her skin against mine, kiss her ass to apologize or whatever the hell ever she demands I do, I walk away. Fuck it hurts; I never, ever, want to experience this again—leaving her behind. But, to avoid further confrontation, I take my spot at the table just as Em does and he launches into my chore for the night.

"The riders are delivering on Trail Street tonight and I need you to keep the five-o distracted. How, I don't care. When, preferably within the hour. I'll compensate you then you can go on your way. Then, when I call for you in the future—and I will—you don't put either one of us through this refusal shit again. Clear? It would be terrible if something happened to that pretty girl you have sitting over there."

My whole body goes rigid, teeth grinding together where they threaten to crack as my overly tense muscles lock tight to prevent me from retaliating. What good would it do anyway? They would hand me my ass on a silver platter. I don't want this 'in,' actually, I want to be so far out of this circle that I'm way in left field.

"Why?" I ask, unsure I truly want the answer he's about to give.

"I've seen you drive. If anyone can keep the cops busy, and get away, it's you. I'm not asking you to do anything illegal, just...keep them occupied however you do."

"You're asking me to put Nadia in a dangerous situation. That doesn't sit right with me, Em."

"I don't give a damn what sits right, I need you to take point on this. So, get your pretty girl, climb in that fucking Matchbox car out there, and do what I asked. Then you can walk away."

Surely he doesn't think I believe that shit, right? It's hard enough for me to trust people under normal circumstances, but in this sort of situation? Like hell. Why can't I tell him no, though?

Her. Because he threatened her. I'll take every threat, every bit of violence, if he just leaves her be.

Glancing over my shoulder, I see Nadia curled up where she sits. Her converse crushing the cushion under her while her arms bind tightly around her bent legs. She looks painfully vulnerable that way, hiding within herself like it will keep the nightmares from toying with her. Still, she's alert with her chin resting on her knees. Keeping her sights on strange people moving around her—in a situation she didn't ask to be a part of.

"Trail Street, you said?" Asking when I give Em my undivided attention.

"Yeah."

"That's precinct three and on the county line. If I'm going to keep them busy, your guys are going to need to move quickly. In and out like wraiths because if I fuck with the pigs too long, they will latch on to me and never let go. And I don't know what's worse, them hunting me for the rest of my life, or you."

"Wise man you are. Here's five bands for good faith. I'll throw on another five when you get the job done."

There's no need for conversation at this point. I don't want the money, I want out of the situation all together, but it's sitting there staring at me and my racing career—the mods and upgrades—they're already burning a hole in my empty pocket. So much can be done to the car if I had ten grand. The circuit would see me too, if the money I needed to buy into bigger races just fell into my lap.

Fuck.

FUCK!

Launching out of my seat, the movement shoves the chair back with so much force it skids across the concrete floor in a nerve grating scrape. Snatching the money from the table, I shove it into my pockets like it's food I've just happened across after starving for days. In a way it is, this is my livelihood sitting there as crisp new Benjamin's—it could cost me everything too.

"I can't fucking believe you!" Nadia shouts at me, furiously latching her harness and tightening the straps. I don't fault her for her anger, this wasn't what she had in mind for her graduation night—frankly it's not what I planned either but life fucks with you that way.

Buckling my own harness, we sit in silence as she stews and I overthink the job. How am I going to execute this and keep her safe? Keep her from cutting me out of her life? Maybe I should add kidnapping to my pending rap sheet and disappear with her despite her wants and desires. Nah, I can't do that, I've fucked up enough as it is. But, I mean, it has its appeal. Handcuff her to me as we sleep, share everything with her—look at me, sounding like a right psychopath.

Cranking the car, she comes to life, music filling the cab once more. That laid back ride we were enjoying earlier? Heh, yeah that shit's long gone now. All that's left is a blanket of tension and animosity, the very same shit I watched her direct at others in the past.

Shifting into reverse, we're out of the parking lot without so much of a fuss despite pulling back onto the road from hell. Each pothole, bump, and dip is less noticeable now that a crater exists between us. When we make it to the highway, Nadia is thrown back in her seat again when Delinquent launches up the on-ramp, zippering into traffic. Weaving between lanes, my feet and hands move through the motions of shifting gears at a subconscious level as I'm too concerned with the rift between us.

"I'm sorry, sweetheart."

"You're sorry?!" There she goes—give me every ounce of your anger, I can handle it.

"Yes, I'm sorry. I hate this ruined your night and there's nothing I can do to get us out of it. I will apologize until I am blue in the face but it doesn't make up for fucking things to hell."

"Whatever he wants you to do, you could have said no. We should have left when I asked to. What are we doing anyway?"

Nadia's venom has simmered a tad, the tone she has is still sharp but she's listening rather than biting my head off—a good sign. Like the disappointment I am, I set her off again.

"We're going to cause a diversion while the riders take care of the real shit. Em is employing my driving, so to say."

"Un-fucking-believable. When we get out of this, you take your ass back to school and leave me the hell alone."

"Oh come on, Nadia. Don't be like that."

On my way to Hell in a hand basket; that's where I'm at right now.

"Don't you dare, Kaleb Reyes. You're lucky I didn't hit the damn pavement and hoof it back to Hazelwood the second you walked away from me. Can you not see how you're fucking with my life? If we get caught, do you know what that means for me? I don't go to juvie, Kaleb! I go to jail. Big jail. Adult jail. I'm eighteen for fucks sake."

"And? I will too." Stay calm, Rey. She's reacting out of fear, not trying to pick a fight.

"What does that matter? Do you know what my dad will do to me if he gets a call from me because I'm locked up? Jesus Christ!"

"You think I don't know? Huh? I've been here through the bulk of it, Nadia. Watched him verbally and emotionally abuse you for years. If you think that's all he's capable of, you're sorely mistaken. So, yes. I know what he will do—what he's capable of. That's why you can't go back, no matter how tonight pans out."

Hate isn't a strong enough word for how I feel about this conversation and the way I've made her feel—trapped.

"So..." She vibrates with disdain. "What's the plan? How are we getting out of this without throwing our lives away for people we don't fucking know?"

As shitty as it sounds, I'm thankful for the safer territory—this I can answer. We can deal with our shit later, right now we have to get through the next half hour, even if it's by the skin of our teeth.

"I'm going to drive, you're going to sit there and hang on. The drop is on Trail Street but we're going to be several miles over on the county line, simply having some fun."

"Fun as in?"

I smile, a full-fledged thousand-watt smile, when she asks. Her inquisitive stare meets mine and then her face drops.

"Oh no." Nadia whispers.

"Oh yes, sweetheart. It's time to drive."

Pressing the clutch, letting off the gas, I drop a gear and the Civic lugs for a second before traction takes and my right foot slams the accelerator. We launch forward, sending the needle into the red zone, and bypass our surroundings in a wicked blur.

Clutch.

Release.

Shift.

Seven...eight thousand.

Clutch.

Release.

Shift.

"Rey!" Nadia gasps. As much as I want to look at her, see the excitement underlining every unsure flick of her stainless-steel eyes, I'm too far in the zone. Adrenaline has taken me captive, I'm a slave to its strength, following every command it barks as we dip and shift through a mirage of cars dotting the highway.

Everything I want out of life is sitting here, in my confident grip, breathing the same air I consume—giving me purpose and life all in one chaotic package.

Then I shift again.

The riders are nowhere to be seen, almost as if they never existed to begin with. Getting to the east side of Detroit was quick, the roads barely bending and twisting, keeping the straightaways open for me to rip down versus banking and feathering the break around slower drivers.

I don't know how I'm going to do this, not when the cops only chase for a few blocks before peeling off—that would require them to do something other than sit and lean against the hood of their cruisers and pester citizens. The sad truth is, stories have come through the grapevine, telling of innocent people being attacked and how officers did nothing. They didn't come to aid, tell others to stop or back up, even when they were questioned or forced to act—taking the victim to jail rather than the perpetrator.

They're as crooked as a snake with the colic. Which makes it difficult to keep their interest, and their pursuit; especially with low-payout crimes like reckless driving. I'll have to get creative if I'm going to keep them on my tail, and a bunch of them at that—long enough for the riders to make their drop and disappear.

Leaving downtown, we're almost at the county line when we zip past a barked cruiser. He flashes his lights briefly but flicks them back off when I touch the accelerator to lure him into a pursuit. Fucker doesn't take the bait.

"Fuck." I grunt.

"What? Can't get them to play with you?" Nadia asks with as much sarcasm as I can handle. "Should have thought about that before you let whatever-his-name-is put you in this position."

"Unless you have a bright idea to get them to engage, we're going to fly through every street here until the damn cows come home, or they chase. Whichever comes first."

I get she's pissed but help, or don't throw fuel on the...

"Sweetheart?"

"What Kaleb." Her response is more of a statement than curiosity.

Oh well.

"Would you climb in the back for me? There's a latch behind the headrest, above the trunk that will lower the back seat. I need you to get something for me."

"I don't know if you noticed but we're driving..." She leans over and looks at the speedometer. "Sixty-five through the city. One pot hole, or one pedestrian, and I'll end up pavement-paint."

"Fine, trade me and I'll do it." My tone mimics the annoyance of hers. She bristles next to me, mouth parting in shock for whatever reason. Those eyes of hers squint with disbelief but I patiently wait for her mouth to work again—speeding up to seventy-five out of spite.

"Are you serious!"

"Nadia, this isn't a game." The words squeeze through my gritted teeth. "Of course I'm serious; I need you to work with me so we can get out of here in one fucking piece. I don't want to do this anymore than you do so please, please sweetheart, either trade me or climb in the back."

Thank god I have all thirty-two teeth because this woman is going to make me pull every one of them by the time I get her to do a damn thing.

After fifty long years, she finally unlatches her harness and practically throws it to the side, one of the metal pieces clacking hard against the window to her right. If she breaks that fucking thing I'm going to spank her until she welts. Shifting onto her knees, she squeezes between our seats, climbing into the back. Her delectable ass and pillowy thighs brush against my right arm before she falls effortlessly onto the bench.

"Thank you. It's on the left side. Plastic. Just wanna…"

"I'm not an idiot."

Wuuusahhhhh, Kaleb.

Her smart fucking mouth makes me want to loop robe around those creamy thighs, spread her apart, and punish her by denying her orgasms. She's going to have to scream and beg for me to stop—the moment we're situated on campus and she's mine for eternity, all bets are off.

Hearing her free the latch behind the seat, she brings it down and starts to climb inside—the road noise is louder now that the thick barrier has been displaced. She shifts around inside, ass waving around and I'm nearly ready to say fuck this drive and eat her alive when I hear her cough and protest.

"What is that smell?"

"Turpentine. Grab it, and some of the rags sitting in that basket."

There's a thud before the tell-tale roll of something heavy into the truck well that clings before Nadia drowns it out with her cussing—more to herself than me. Whatever she knocked over, which I have an idea, consumes more of her time when she chases it down and puts it back. Following her muted tirade, my eyes rake over her in the rear-view mirror, one more time when she wiggles out from the loud trunk.

Plopping down, she briefly looks out the window and the side view mirror. The sidewalks are decorated with never-ending advertisements for skyrise apartments and breakthrough medical treatment. Beyond them are benches, trees, bus stops, and city trash cans that have seen better days.

Is…is she scouting the area?

The thought makes me grin, even with the annoyance hanging between us. Finally she looks at me and holds up the tin container of turpentine, in her other hand a dinghy-red mechanics rag.

"The hell am I supposed to do with this?"

Approaching a red light, I downshift and come to a stop, idling between a champagne-colored Cadillac Escalade and a bright red Dodge Neon—the hum of the Civic reverberates against them, amplifying the purr. My fingers ache so bad I fear they may snap from how hard I have been handling the steering wheel. Prying them away from the leather, and taking the rags from her, I shake them. It takes me just a few seconds to isolate a corer, and motion for the metal jug.

"Pop the lid, sweetheart. Then shove this inside of it and give it a little shake. You want the liquid to soak into the rag or it won't work right."

Green flares across the hood when the traffic light switches, distracting me from her and her newfound task. Taking a left, I pull a U-turn at the light and head back down the same route, to the officer who flashed his lights at me.

"Okay, now what?"

Leaning to the left, I pull my zippo from my pocket and flick it open. The metal lid makes that famous sound when I pass it to her.

"We're going to light it up."

I'm surprised by the expression that comes over her face—a mask sliding into place on my deviant...my violent little minx.

"And where exactly are we going to do that?"

Intrigued, I smirk at her. "Anywhere you want."

Clenching the lighter now, her left thumb brushes back and forth along the harsh grooves of the striker when she starts searching for a target. Me?

I accelerate faster, hoping and praying I get to the true intended recipient before she makes any other fun decisions. If we didn't already have something important to do, I'd let her throw that damn thing anywhere, but alas, I need it as much as I need her.

"Alright." That word—it eases from her lips all smooth and silk-like. What I'd give to taste it, to lick it off those lush pouts, and feed it right back to her on the tip of my tongue. Wrenching my mind out of the gutter, I press the switch on my door to lower her window down. Thinking I would need to make another U-turn at the next light to reach the officer, Nadia surprises me by climbing out of the window and sitting on the ledge—so much for being scared of removing her harness at sixty-five miles an hour.

Flick, flick, flick. She strikes the lighter then goes quiet right as *Fire Woman* cues up on the radio, the irony making me chuckle. With a slight jerk of my wrist, we swerve closer to the officer who is finally interested in our summertime shenanigans.

Then? My diabolica throws the canister at the officer's windshield and it erupts in flames.

"That's my fucking girl!"

CHAPTER EIGHT

"Oh fuck! Oh fuck, oh fuck, Kaleb!" She squeals.

Nothing stops me from laughing at her anxious shouts, or the way she's now death gripping the 'oh shit' handle above her window. Clinging to the damn thing like a life raft while she jolts abruptly in her chair from the hella rough get away—lacking any sort of finesse. Her involvement though? I'm impressed as fuck, I didn't think she had it in her for one. Two, I had no idea it would turn me on as much as it has.

My foot has the accelerator crushed to the floor, any harder and I'm going to break through the aluminum frame and hit the pavement racing beneath us. Red and blue lights are flashing behind us in multiple pairs, one directly behind and two flanking him. I'm not sure how many other patrol vehicles there are but I'll be damned if I'm not testing every bit of athletic ability this car has to offer. I bob and weave through traffic while a few vehicles try, and nearly fail, to get out of the way before we fly past them.

Sirens screech angrily behind us when we fly through another intersection. I rip the wheel to the right to circle back around and almost toss Nadia onto the center console. It's shitty work but serves a purpose, this running in circles, keeps the cops busy, us out of jail, and gives the riders what time they need to finish their drop.

While I don't encourage criminal activity, I'm having more fun blazing through downtown with Nadia by my side than I think we would have had sitting under the stars—thank God I turned right and came to the city; consequences be damned.

While the squad cars are not gaining on us, it won't be too much longer before my fuel gauge starts to dip. When you drive like a bat out of hell, it plows through your reserves pretty fast and, though the officers have bigger vehicles, they likely have more-full tanks. Therefore, I need to be strategic in our getaway—or our cat and mouse game, whatever.

Nestled on both sides of the steering wheel are small red buttons that I rarely ever use on the street, typically saving them for the track, but between you and me, this calls for it. Besides, I really want to see what sort of reaction I can get out of Nadia when we smoke the pigs behind us. Or how hard it's going to be to comprehend Detroit's business district as it blurs outside of our windows.

"Nadia, seatbelt. Now." Demanding and needing her strapped in safely before I push the damn NOS release; thankful when she doesn't hesitate. She's shaking and fumbling around so much she's struggling to get it together. The harness isn't the most confusing contraption but when you're running on fear and excitement, it does get more difficult than it needs to be. Finally I hear it, the clink of clasping metal and the belt's low rasp when she yanks it hard and secures herself into place.

As soon as she stills, her hands finding the console and the door handle, my thumbs press down on the small red rubber-coated buttons, launching

Delinquent even faster. Nadia gasps when she's thrown back in her seat, her hands shoot to the straps restraining her shoulders and hold on to them until her fingers begin to pale from her desperate grip.

Instantly, the sights and sounds of the city morph into a blur. Colors blending together and streaking past the tinted windows, a roar of air rushing half in and half out of the same open space, and underneath it all, Nadia's giggles. Every damn ounce of me wants to look over, to see that beautiful smile I know she is capable of, to witness joy and excitement on her face at this exact moment. This is getting to her, it's bringing her out of her safe shell and damn, it makes me feel good.

I can't however, I won't, not until we are out of here and safe. One wrong move: a pedestrian crossing the road, another cop showing up ahead of us and throwing down spikes, hell even a newspaper catching on the windshield and I would kill her. That can never happen. Focus—glide left, ease right through both moving and stand-still traffic.

More cruisers join the ones behind us as we rocket past them at intersections, their lights a blaze of purple by the time our brains process the color change. This shit is surreal. There's no fucking way I'm in a high-speed chase in Detroit with Nadia in the car. The high-stakes, fear, unknown, the unpredictability of the whole ordeal has me ready to choke. We are though. Both of us are cocooned in a fiberglass and aluminum torpedo with nothing between us except shit I'm too afraid to say and the scream of eighty's hair metal.

Red and blue lights steadily flicker while headlights beam brightly through the ever-increasing gap—the cruisers unable to keep up with the new speeds we're reaching. In a split second, I take a quick peek at the speedometer and other gauges, noting one hundred and twenty-seven miles an hour—creeping on one twenty-eight. There is no doubt in my mind the car will go faster, I'm only biding my time; this also isn't the place with too many variables and elements that could bring everything crashing down.

Highway signs are beginning to pop up on the intersection poles, directing us to it, where we will really disappear and escape the police. From my jacket pocket, my phone tings—Emmett. I don't have to look to know what it's saying, we're done, the riders are finished with their drop and we are free to get the hell out of dodge.

"Sweetheart?"

"Y...yeah?" Nadia shudders out a breath.

"What do you say, we get lost?"

"Are, are you done here? We can go?"

"Yes. Give me the word and I'll lose them then it will be just you and me."

A smile comes to my face when Nadia pauses, taking her time to contemplate if she's ready to leave or not, all while we continue to actively break the law. Which reminds me, I'll need to get license plate replacements when Zap and I return to campus—the cops have had plenty of time to pull my information up and might have already requested a warrant from a judge. I suppose Em better e ready to lawyer me the fuck up because I refuse to relinquish my racing future, or one with Nadia, to be on the run for his ass.

After what feels like an eternity, we both spot the on-ramp. That's when she decides to give me an answer, when I was ready to decide for her.

"Smoke 'em, Rey."

"Yes ma'am." Heat settles bone deep into my tone. I'm fighting something fierce within me, it's trying to burn its way out while I swallow it down. Unease? No. Worry? Hell naw. I don't know how to explain it, all I know is it's devouring me from the inside out.

The on-ramp is officially in my sights and I am locked on it like some sort of fighter-jet pilot. It's my target. The goal is to get to it faster than we've been going and find a big enough space in traffic to safely merge, then put even more distance between us and Detroit's not-so-finest.

Flicking my eyes ahead, I hunt for the perfect spot as rubber meets the ramp's pavement, then we squeeze into the smallest opening between two tractor-trailers within seconds. Glancing, ensuring my blind spots are clear, we move into the next lane over—manipulating the traffic to our benefit. The moment cop lights appear again, I'm jamming the second NOS button and like a space shuttle, we're out of here.

Mile after mile, Detroit disappears behind us. The blinding lights finally fade—neon giving way to the darkness of night; stars dot the atmosphere like tiny sparkling pinholes. With the windows down it's easier to catch them flickering in the corner of my eyes, along with Nadia's hair whipping around in the rough air. She's quiet, the soft rasp of her voice no longer harmonizing with the music pouring through the system—admiring the shadows consuming the land on her side of the highway.

We're halfway between New Baltimore and Port Huron now. I took the off ramp a few miles back and moved onto the backroads—searching for a place to hide out for a bit and let the heat from the city die down.

It's more peaceful out here, which I prefer, and truthfully I want alone time with her. Park somewhere we can talk undisturbed, and listen to music, maybe even daydream about what's next in her life—convince her to leave Hazelwood behind and be with me. Groveling too, there's not much in this world I won't do for her and if she demands that I crawl across God's green Earth to apologize for ruining her night by kissing the toe of her shoe, I will.

Finding an overgrown drive and letting off of the gas pedal, we slow down before I ease on the break and creep off the black-top. We crawl down a gravel road, nestled in darkness and overseen by wildlife. Even the trees protect this spot by reaching over the road while some branches dip dangerously close to the top of the car. Thankfully the small fingerling twigs and leaves never officially touch the paint. Beyond our windows, I can hear a low crunch and crackle remixing with shifting rocks as the tires roll over debris. Deeper and deeper we go, disappearing into the night.

From here, I notice a pull-off on my left. I roll past then stop and reverse far enough down the drive where only the headlights are sticking out, they won't be noticeable once I flip them off and leave only the radio playing.

Parked, I reach and turn the dial down some then unbuckle my harness—Nadia follows suit. The only other noise interrupting the playing is the soft clinks of metal and our gentle movements. Nervousness hits me with the weight of a freight train. After the shit we've gone through tonight, and having known her for a few years, there's no damn reason I should be feeling this way. I know her. She knows me. We're...*friends*. Not if I have anything to fucking say about it, not after tonight.

"C'mere," I drawl, reaching for her hand to help her move over; color me surprised when she doesn't hesitate.

Giving her time to settle, her legs stretch over the console as my left arm curls around her waist, stopping her from putting too much weight on the door and hurting her back. I like her center, right on the middle of my lap, having her pressed against me like I'm property and the faint scent of her body wash permeating my clothes. She likely has no clue but she's my warding, scaring people away who try to get within an arm's length of me. Tugging her slightly, my right hand splays across the outer side of her left thigh and tightens—kneading her flesh.

I want to lean in, to take her lips against mine and still a kiss I'm dying for, or ten, hell let's make it twenty. However many she's willing to part with to save a lonely soul like mine. Despite it all, she's going to have to close the space—the ball is finally in her field.

"I'm sorry about tonight. It's not what I had planned at all."

Growing a pair, I look at her, our displaced heights giving her a few inches now that she's perched on my lap like the goddess she is, taking claim of the dominion that is rightfully hers. Within seconds I'm sucked in by her sterling silver eyes, the words I had loaded on the tip of my tongue instantly die there. Dark strands of windblown hair are framing her face, some hanging and curling in softly swept spirals that rest at the jumping pulse of her neck. Greedily, I squeeze her thigh again, both hands yanking her impossibly closer.

"S...say something." Whispering into the sparse space between us.

When she doesn't, my heart leaps into my throat. I don't know what to do, what to say, maybe I fucked everything up tonight and there's no coming back from it. Everything I've worked for, the years I've waited to be with her, the decisions I made to ensure I can take her back to campus with me—gone. It's over. Having to see the livelihood of unsavory people and getting caught up in it, was all it took for her to run the opposite direction.

Nadia has dealt with so much emotional and mental torment from her old man and I should have known better. I threw her freedom on the chopping block right when she was at the custom of having it all—this is the price I'm paying now. *Her.* There's no way I can apologize my way out of this fuckup, and knowing that has my stomach plummeting. Still, my pleading mouth opens.

"Nadia, please. You've got to believe..." the words fall silent as she pushes a digit against my lips.

"Don't," she stops me. "I forgive you, just, stop. You don't have to do that. Not with me, not ever."

"Sweetheart, I..."

Snapping my mouth closed, I fight the urge in me and don't do it again. Shifting my hands, pulling her upper body to mine, both of my arms wrap around her, hugging her to me. Then I do something I have wanted to do every night since she broke up with me; bury my nose into her wild hair and suck in the deepest, lung exploding, breath I can manage.

"Missed you so much. You know that? Fucking sucks in the city without you."

Not only can I smell her, feel her, but I've intruded into her bubble so deep I can hear her heart pattering near my face.

Lub-dub lub-dub lub-dub.

Just when I thought she's going to keep all of those feelings of hers wrapped up tight and boxed in cement, she opens up.

"I missed you too, more than I should have." Her voice thick and smokey as she murmurs close to me.

Breaking away, and forgoing the idea of waiting for her to close the distance, I steal her. Crashing my lips to her gloss-coated ones until her breath hitches and her body melts on my lap. I'm ready to fall apart at the seams, crumble to the shadows of perdition, burst into dust when her arms coil over my shoulders and jerk me closer. Our teeth click from the deepened kiss then she opens without my prompting, I take the bait because I'm a fucking sucker for her.

My life hasn't been exciting other than racing here or there. I'm not the smartest guy, I don't have money. And football? Meh. College is a simple stepping stone and an accomplishment for Ma, rather than myself. This girl though, no...this woman, is the most important part of me that I'll never let go of. Nadia is my excitement, she's the light that brings out the freckles across my face, the sun that makes my eyes burn gold, and the one I'll spend the rest of my life worshiping.

"I love you," I stutter into her mouth. Releasing her only to cradle her face for a moment, slowing down the kiss. "I want you." My tongue caresses hers, memorizing the softness of her pouts and the sharp way she stops breathing. "I need you." The last words fall from my lips; she catches between her teeth, pinching them into my bottom one then scrapes them away from the tender skin—swallowing them whole.

Without letting her get a word in, terrified she will turn me down, I kiss her harder. She's burning on my lap—pure fire scorching me through denim as if it is litmus paper, spurring me on and on.

Squirming and fucking giggling now—she pants against my lips, the bashful sound barely breaking past the obsession taking root.

"Mmm, you laughing at me, sweetheart?"

"M...maybe. What you g...going to do about it?" Even now she teases me, giddy, taunting, and making me work for the privilege to exist in her orbit.

Escaping her deliciously kiss-swollen lips, she hovers those few inches over me, knowing she has all the power to bless or condemn me if she so chooses. What better way to get back at her, than play with each of her sensitive nerves. Sliding a hand down, rough fingertips graze the bare skin of her arm where the finest little hairs stand on end in a parade. Bypassing her hand, my fingers ease further down to her leg—where I may flirt with the hem of her shorts. Weaving my rough touch slowly in and out from under it at random, igniting another blaze.

"That's not very nice of you. Kicking me when I'm trying to tell you you're coming home with me. Not just for tonight though, not for the weekend or the summer, forever."

Down the length of her leg I go, around to the back of her thigh, through the ditch of her knee to her calf, and further until the ridge of her ankle bone combats the firmness of my touch. Up this time, along her shin, kneecap, then she parts her thighs and I groan.

"F...fucking hell."

Adrenaline is surging through me, on a mission with a few other choice endorphins, kickstarting my heart.

"Forever?" Her lips caress the three syllables while staring at me so hard I swear I'm made of glass and might break under her scrutiny.

"Yes," Answering confidently. "Forever. You have until the end of the weekend to enjoy your graduation and then I'll be back on Monday with boxes. You're leaving with me. If you want to take time off from school to figure out what works for you, take it. If you decide to say 'fuck your opinion' and start college, I'll support your decision—from our place."

I'm proud of myself for getting all of that out without stuttering like an idiot. I mean every damn word, she will be with me and free from her dad before he manages to get his nasty ass home from work. There's even the choice for her to go no-contact if she wishes, I won't push it on her. The asshole will show more of his true colors once he realizes she's gone and not hanging out with her friends where he can show up and bully her back to the house. By then, she's all mine and there's not a fucking thing Gene can do about it.

"Is that what you think I want, Kaleb? To run away with you? Uproot everything I know and depend on another man to take care of me?"

"Yes. You deserve a better life and I promise to give it to you. Hazelwood will crush you like it does everyone else. There's no amount of thriving or being happy there—you'll end up another statistic and I can't have that. I don't give a damn how selfish it sounds, you're not living this way anymore."

All while I'm spilling my ill-expressed hopes and dreams to her, my hand travels up her frame back to her face. There's no stopping me from roughing a thumb against her bottom lip and watching it blush—she sure as fuck doesn't. The way she talks, the tone, the intentional way she moves through life, has me momentarily distracted but I pick up her words anyway.

"What did you say?" Catching her throat with a firm grip, I squeeze, daring her to repeat the shit she had the nerve to say.

"M...make m...me."

CHAPTER NINE

N adia's heart is beating wildly in my hand, her pulse is directly be- neath my fingers with my thumb feathering on the other side of her neck—preventing her from moving again. Not while I'm starving for her, not when she's squirming on my lap and every brain cell I have has taken a sudden vacation.

I want her, I need her. I...fuck, I'm so gone.

Crushing my lips to hers again, our foreheads meet with the same level of desperation, all while I grind my hips against her ass. Rough gasps of breath rush through my nose, fighting the eagerness pulling me apart, so I don't make some rookie-ass mistake and pass out on the girl I'd conquer empires for. For years I've told everyone brave enough to ask who she belonged to, who I needed more than the blood coursing through my veins; truthfully? I belong to her. She sank her claws into me a long time ago, back when she told me to kick rocks, as if she isn't the earth beneath them, knocking me off my feet. Here she is again, coiling her constricting chains around me—capturing my love, my mind, my soul.

The second she opens her lush lips, I dive in. Tongue slipping into the heat of her mouth, tasting her silent pleading, teasing her until she whines and the vibration tickles my palm. I can't stop myself from kissing her, slow and deep, the way I plan to for the rest of our lives as I hold her in place by her thin neck. Controlling the moment because the second I let her go, a new kind of blaze will scorch the both of us.

"R...rey." My name's a desperate breath stolen from my mouth that she inhales.

"What... what is it, sweetheart?"

Please don't talk. It will break me if this ends.

When words fail her, she answers me by rocking her curvy hips back and forth instead—I'm about to lose my fucking mind. As needy as I am for her, seeking and silently begging for the very thing her mouth is too shy to ask for, I have to hear her say it. Not only because I want to make sure she's as hungry for me as I am for her, but because it strokes my ego a little bit and makes me hard as fuck when her mouth is filthy.

"Mmm, words, Nadia. Tell me what you're hunting for; wiggling around like that."

Stopping her motions, my free hand dips under her shirt and slides up to her waist, the ghost of her rib bone firm and unforgiving under my roughened fingertips. She doesn't answer, not yet, but we will work on that—she will learn to beg. And plead. And scream before I let her out of this fucking car.

It might have been a few years since we lost our virginities to one another but I've done my research—studied a darker side of pleasure that she seems to like, given the way she's rutting on my lap. After everything, I still discover something new about her that convinces the heavens made her specifically for me.

We'll learn all sorts of things together—deviant.

"Come on, sweetheart. If you don't tell me, I'll stop and we both know that's not what you want, now is it?"

"N...nuh," she protests with a pout.

"Wordssss, Nadia," I warn, sliding my hand higher, around her ribcage to tease the swell of her under-bust. Her delicious nipples pebbling under her bra once I decide to tease one and brush my thumb over it. Right when she's starting to slip, I stop and she whines.

"M...more, please. I..."

There we go, I almost prompt her for more but I'll wait. Giving her space, I wait for her to put her head back on straight; expecting her to tell me she's mine and she wants this as much as I do. That she will run away with me and never look back.

"Want you. It's been so, so long."

"That so? You mean to tell me, you've waited for me like I've waited for you?" Tilting, my nose brushes the edge of her jawline, roaming up to her ear to hear me clearly the next time I speak.

"Yessss. I've waited. Couldn't...couldn't let anyone else touch me. M...made my skin crawl."

"Mmmhm, what else? Tell me everything, Nadia. What I've missed these years and I don't mean our dates, the nights we would hang out and do nothing but watch dry-TV, or your public life. I want your deep thoughts, sweetheart. Each and every one of them."

"Kaleb—I couldn't. Never. I tried once, thinking of you and it, it felt wrong. You. I..."

"Couldn't what?"

Easing my fingers under her bra, she goes rigid but I squeeze the sides of her neck to calm her. She's doing so good, I need the rest of what she's trying to say. The faster, the better, because I'm about to lose my load before ever getting inside of her.

"Touch myself." Nadia answers and her skin flames—blushing.

I stop immediately, looking at her in absolute awe at her confession. Admiring and feral at the same damn time. Technically, what I'm about to do is manipulative, she's under the influence of endorphins and lust, but I know what's in my Diabolica's heart.

"Run away with me." I whisper into her ear, my fingers catch a nipple and pinch—still as sensitive as ever, her hips bucking, seeking relief. She's always liked a little pain, and while it surprised me at first, I now know why. My girl finds solace in feeling the hole in her chest disappear when pain erupts across her sweet skin, craving the release from life, and responsibility even if it's only for a moment. She has trauma, her mother leaving, a broken childhood, a piece of shit father—this helps her process in a healthy way before she's allowed to forget. Finally, words slip past her trembling lips and make me unfathomably happy.

"O-okay. I'll run away with you."

Not requiring anything else, my hand leaves her throat to grab her chin, where I can kiss her again. All of my love pours into it, every brush of my tongue giving her a taste of just how much she completes me. My opposite hand is on a mission, fisting the front of her bra and yanking it down until it catches under her breast. Her hardening nipples lift the black fabric enough where the moonlight catches on them through the windshield.

Ravenously, I pull away from her lips and yank her shirt up. I need to see them—those dusky pink peaks I've not tasted in years. Throwing her shirt into the passenger seat, my mouth is on her, drawing the left into the heat, and swirling my tongue around it. Her whimpers are music to my ears. Soft huffs join them when she works to push her chest closer to me and dig her fingers into my cropped hair.

Yesssss, sweetheart.

Scraping my teeth over her sensitive flesh, her nipple pops free. The other's already waiting for the same treatment, which I won't deny her when she's being so good for me. This time she groans, a muted thud providing backdrop when her head tilts to the window behind her. I swap back and forth a few times, kissing along the upper swell and delivering bites at random, forcing her skin to pucker with both anger and lust.

"Unbutton your shorts, and lift up."

Unraveling my arms, I shoulder off my jacket, practically ripping my shirt off next. Inch after inch of caramel colored skin contrasts her paler flesh in the cosmic light. Right as she lifts, I'm unbuckling my belt and driving down my zipper—too excited, too desperate for her.

I hook my fingers behind the waistband of her shorts within seconds, impatient as ever to have her wrapped around my cock, but I'm not so bold to yank them and jerk her around the car's small interior. Guiding them down the long lines of her legs, I fling them to the side where they join our shirts on the other seat–burning me alive when she rests her bare ass on my lap again.

Fuckin' hell.

The way she tastes resides in a memory, and will remain there, for now. Without enough room for me to lay her out, I'll have to wait before I can spread her wide enough to feast on her until her cries pierce my ears. To top it off, she also doesn't have the space to swallow me down the way I fucking love—we'll have plenty of time later. Right now is about stoking this inferno, making her come all over my cock, and weld her to me once and for all.

This time, she kisses me—taking matters into her own hands—thrusting her tongue into my mouth with greed. Containing my chuckle is a fool's errand when it rumbles and evolves into something more primal, my hand sliding down the front of her underwear to find her wet and throbbing.

Jesus Christ.

"Mmm, sweetheart, that's exactly what I was hoping for. Fucking drenched."

Nadia tries to pop off, probably a smart-ass retort, but I catch her before she's able to. Easing two fingers into her, I revel like a fucking king when she moans and tightens around them. If she thinks clamping down is going to stop me, she has another thing coming. Especially when my fingers curl up into the soft, spongy, spot behind her pubic bone that makes her tremble.

At some point, she wound an arm behind my neck for leverage. Her sharp nails begin to dig into the shoulder cap with every stroke of her g-spot. It's delicious, the pain—a weak bite through the muscle spurring me on rather than slowing my touch. Between the lines, however, it reminds me how beautifully she's going to come apart for me. How she will show me that pleasure-drunken side she's reserved for me, and me alone. Then, beneath it all, she's still her. All fight, barely any play, and when she does bloom, she's dangerous. Even I'm not safe because living on the edge is exactly what we both thirst for.

Fighting her strength, I slide my fingers in and out, nearly leaving her empty, making her whine before thrusting them back in. Poor thing is shaking already, suppose I could give her a few precious seconds to ready herself–nah. Stroking a few more times, I repeat the same motion but rougher; over and over until her arousal finally soaks through the front of my boxers.

Flattening the heel of my palm to her pulsing clit, my pointer finger eases out, trading with my ring finger. All while I pepper open mouth kisses up and down her neck, punctuating a few of them with a bite here and there. We're both already panting, keyed up and so fucking deep in the thick of it, there's no way in hell we'll resurface before we drown.

Without warning, I jerk my arm, stopping when she gasps, testing the waters so to speak. Tensing, she grinds her ass down onto my too-hard cock making me see stars. Denying her for a few labored breaths, I make her wait, wanting her so fucking wound up she comes all over my dick before I'm remotely close to finishing with her.

One Mississippi, two Mississippi.

Thrusting again, she coats my hand in her delicious arousal—can't wait to suck her off my fingers before sinking into her. Curl my tongue around all three digits, lap her sweet taste from every raised print pad and the ditch between each of them. Before calling it quits, and doing the damn thing anyway, her thighs part further as she bucks forward–my fingers invading deeper into her slick pussy.

Perfect, so goddamn perfect.

A stunning shade of pink has bloomed beneath her ear, creeping down her neck into the divots of her clavicles where it pools like summertime sweat.

There's nothing stopping me, not life, not people, not even the law chasing us earlier—absolutely nothing is in the way of me branding her skin with the crescent moon shaped curve of my bite. I refuse to resist anymore, she will wear me several times over before I take her home.

Baring my teeth, I bite down on the side of her neck until she screams out, bucking her hips desperately—so damn close she's fluttering around my fingers. Milking at them with long hard pulls that have me slowing my pace but I can't do that to her. I can't torture her like this, egg her on, make her beg and plead, promise me things she might not have to give then leave her hanging.

On the other hand, I could. I'll confuse her body, make her ache and associate me with pleasure rather than simply being her friend—especially now that we are free to be involved. It's a profound idea, having her as obsessed with me as I am with her. Then again, I can wait and torment her another day. If I don't get inside of her, if I don't make her unravel at the seams, we both might lose our ever-loving minds, and two love-drunk insane people never turn out right. I mean, look at Bonnie and Clyde or Antony and Cleopatra.

I could be nice, let her have this one orgasm before she's given another, then another, and countless more after tonight. Decisions, decisions.

Thrusting my fingers deep into her, my middle gently strokes her cervix at the same time my pointer mimics the motion against her g-spot. And forget her clit? Hell no, my thumb's focused on it, tight slow circles atop of her hood as I manipulate every fucking nerve ending she has. Listening to her cry, and pant, and writhe to escape.

"Kaleb! Please, fuck. Don't... stop. Oh—OH FUCK!"

Nadia almost launches her head back to the window but I'm careful, shifting her just in time for her to miss it and still scream through the violent bucking of her curvy hips. Riding my hand, drenching me in her release as the smooth fabric of my boxers struggle to absorb all she gives me—leaving her scent lingering in my clothes.

"That's it, sweetheart. So fucking pretty when you come for me. Tell me you want another and I'll give it to you; I'll fuck every inch of my cock into this cunt until you're drunk and your pussy chokes the cum out of me."

Her beautiful silver eyes are blown out and heavily armored with her barely painted eyelids. Still, she stares down at where I'm determined to draw out each and every shudder her sensitive body offers.

"M...more. P...please Kaleb."

Whatever my girl wants, she gets. Keeping my fingers plunged inside of her, I shift to escape my confining boxers—freeing my dick with a gasp of my own. Precum leaks from the flustered and flared tip, the foreskin no longer protecting my glands as hard as I am. Settling her down, the last few inches of me stick out freely between her thighs. Pulling my fingers free, she pouts at the emptiness that I silence when I rock up to her.

"Just a second," my breathy-words flood the side of her neck and jaw. It takes me little time to find a condom in the center console, rip open the aluminum packaging, and roll it on. In the past I gave her the opportunity to do this, she enjoyed it, learning how to do things that set us both on edge–right now, I'm too impatient. Rolling the cream-colored rubber down to the last centimeter or so of my cock, I line up with her pulsating cunt and push inside. Grabbing her hips, I drag her down onto me, filling her to the brim.

Jesus Christ almighty. Stop Kaleb, stop or you're going to bust right now.

She feels so fucking good, just how I remember. Snug, but not so tight it hurts, slick with need, taking me with ease despite the pressure of stretching her. Greedily capturing her lips, it's my turn to moan–it's heady and hopeless pouring into her mouth.

Limited on space, I reach for the release between my seat and the door and force the seat to recline; awarding me an unobstructed view of Nadia—well almost. Without slipping out, I turn her, positioning her against the steering wheel—uncomfortable I am sure—and help her bracket her feet on both sides of my waist. Spreading her wider, she hovers a few inches over me as I help support her by holding her up by her creamy thighs. Finally, I buck two, three, urgent times.

"Ask for it again, sweetheart. Do it. Ask for your cock."

The brat forces herself down to my hilt then lifts, the condom glistening with her slick release when she threatens me by rising until only my tip remains inside of her.

"Don't you fucking do it, Nadia. Not tonight. I need you too bad."

"Then you beg. Beg to fuck me senseless, Kaleb. You want this pussy, then you say please."

What the hell is she doing to me? I ask myself as my cock jumps, taking it upon itself to try and coerce her into slamming down on me. She's fucking mine, has been from the get go and will be mine even when she's hovering over me and keeping me from being balls deep inside of her. I'm ready to reach up, grab her by the damn throat and force her onto me but I'm not an ass–if she wants me to beg, then I'll beg.

"Please, sweetheart. May I, please, fuck this beautiful cunt?"

Dropping my head back, I grip her thighs until the joints in my fingers ache, the devil practically falls and impales herself on me. Losing my hold,

I swap with her waist, it's not as firm as her hips but I love how she squeezes between my fingers in softer areas. Steadying her over me I take the opportunity to snap my hips forward and bury myself several times before she tries to take control again. Drowning out the syrupy drawl of her moan each time my sack and the tops of my thighs smack against her.

So fucking good, this—this is what I've waited so long for, what I'm grateful for every damn day and will be for the rest of my life.

Needing to see her, to watch my dick take her apart, I tilt my head again. Lust-heavy eyes focus on where we're meeting, eating up the sight of me stretching her open—of her swollen clit begging for its own attention. Too bad, I'm not letting go of her right now. Instead, I take her throat anyway, grasping, and cutting off the breath she's not allowed to steal without permission, then I yank her to me. Changing the angle, she's rubbing herself on my groin now while I'm surging in and out of her tight grip.

"So per...fect." Replacing my breath with her own for another kiss. She responds by invading my mouth, muting me.

That's it, stingy thing.

There's no stopping us—we're ravenous for this. The connection, being seen, being appreciated for who we are without the expectations of our families. There's no grade point averages or job requirements here, just pure fucking lust and a love that will outlast time.

Pressure's building low in my stomach, running me along with the burn of my exerted muscles, delivering a heady cocktail to my mind and body.

She fits me perfectly. The flare of her hips below my hand, her chest pressed flat to mine, the exact size of her neck fitting in my grip, then the way I slot between her thighs like we were formed from matching molds.

I can't take it anymore—thrusting harder, more desperate, and losing my steady rhythm, my orgasm rushes towards me. If I have anything to say about it, she's going too, we're falling over this together. Hand in hand, soul with soul.

Binding both arms around her, I pant against her neck. "Please come with me, Nadia. Show me who owns me."

One, two, three more thrusts and she screams. Her orgasm triggers mine, shoving as far into her spasming pussy, I moan into her shoulder. Filling the condom with spurt after spurt of hot cum, giving myself to the only woman I've ever wanted.

CHAPTER TEN

The leather's sticking to me; it's not necessarily uncomfortable though. We shimmied into the back seat before I lost all of my starch and gave out under her. It's strange, as I'm normally in the front seat rather than laying in the back. But it feels good here with her weight resting firmly against mine. She's sticking to me too, with our bare chests skin-to-skin. Gently, my fingers glide up and down her spine–taking count of each vertebrae along her lumbar and thoracic zones.

Our breathing has synced up; each of her soft exhales fog warmly across my flesh while I graze her cheek with my opposite thumb. Holding her in ways I've fantasized about—both with tenderness and hunger.

Tightening for a moment, I shift subtly and lift my left leg then rest it on the side of the backrest of the backseat—too damn tall to be fucking in a car but it's a small price to pay. Nadia murmurs incoherently, the sweet contented sound blending with *Stairway to Heaven* as it plays faintly through the speakers—almost choking me with sentimentality.

"You alright, sweetheart?"

I know she's alright, I still need to hear her say it. Give me peace of mind after the insane evening we've had, and the role she played—blew my mind, no pun intended. Never would've guessed how much of a firebug she is. Hell, she probably doesn't realize it either but that fucker is loitering inside of her, squatting, waiting to show its ugly head again. If I know anything about Nadia, this is only the beginning. She doesn't do things halfway, it's all or none. Which you would be a damn fool not to admire about her.

"Hey," prompting her again, I tilt her chin to see her better. I have to bite the inside of my lip when I get a good look at her—the poor thing is blissed out. Eyes heavy, cheeks still stained a heated pink, lips so kiss-swollen I'm sure they hurt. Unfortunately for her, that doesn't stop me from brushing my thumb across them, the rough callous pushing the reddened cushion to the side.

"Hey, beautiful girl."

"Mmm."

A gentle chuckle jolts my chest, part of me knows I shouldn't laugh at her but it's impossible to stop. Elation exists unapologetically in every ounce of my body and she's the entire damn reason. If she can't see more than a few inches in front of her, at least she can hear the dumb ass smirk on my face—pride. *Glutinous pride.*

"Need to know you're alright, give me more than a contented murmur."

"Mmm." She answers me again.

"Brat." I reply then land a series of quick slaps down on her bare ass until her teasing turns into a shout.

"Kaleb!"

"That's better, not what I was looking for but yelling my name is an acceptable alternative. It sounds good rolling out all sex-dazed and whatnot."

"You...'re a jerk." Nadia groans, pulling away from my thumb and laying her head back down where her ear almost suctions to it—listening to the low thuds of the heart she's enslaved.

"A handsome one that hopefully just made up for ruining your graduation night."

"Still in the doghouse, just renting though. Not living."

That chuckle from before? A full laugh now, one that starts deep in my torso before rumbling out and creating a mini earthquake for the woman laying atop of me. The curl of her lips warms my heart–well fucked, relaxed, and simply existing. Exactly how it should be, us facing the rest of the world together.

"I missed this, you know. You remember the first time I snuck in your window? Almost busted my ass when my jacket got caught on the nail your dad used to board it up from the outside."

She doesn't say anything for a few seconds then finally adds in. "Yeah, and you blamed me for the torn leather for two weeks."

"Three weeks, but yeah. This reminds me of that night. And the one where we managed to climb on the rooftop and watch the meteor shower. What movie were we trying to watch on that old DVD player I stole from, damnit, what was his name in school? Leon, Larry..."

"Levi," she cuts me off. "*Dazed and Confused.*"

"Yeah, that's right, and Levi. What happened to him?"

"He moved after you graduated, somewhere down south I think. Missouri, Oklahoma, Texas, hell if I know where."

"You must keep up with him if you have a general idea where he went." Probing her for information, hoping to see just how close she might have gotten with someone else while I was away. The not-so-jolly green monster is frolicking around the inside of my head, goading me by having me overthink shit. Jealousy is a motherfucker, I tell you. I've watched my boys with girls in college, and while I wasn't jealous of them specifically, I was envious of what they had–allowed to do the things that I desperately craved with Nadia.

Now though? I'm curious to know if someone else tickled her fancy since the last night I held her. If someone else did, I'm going to make a run before the weekend is through, break their hands and sever whatever part of them touched her in my absence.

"Maybe I do. Maybe he sends me love messages through emails with virtual flowers."

There's no damn way she's being serious right now. Not laying against me like this, holed up in my car, naked chest to chest, having moaned from coming on my cock, no—nope—she's got to be fucking with me...right?

She must sense the turmoil bulldozing my emotions because she sits up. Her hair's in a tangly mess, hanging past her shoulders in swaths that accentuate her dusky-colored nipples. Looking at her at this moment, I'm unworthy. There's no damn way I got lucky enough in life to have this stunning woman sitting on me the way she is, exposed and comfortable enough in her skin to make me question my place in her life.

"You have a problem with that? Someone swooning over me, wanting to take me on candle lit dinners, long walks on the beach with sand between my toes, paint murals at church, and host dinner parties?"

"Bet your ass I have a damn problem with that." Snapping my reply, the anger she's expertly stoking in me competes with the torch Prometheus gifted to humans so the world no longer had to live in darkness. The same heat that's turning my ears red and crawling up my neck with, you guessed it, jealousy.

How fucking dare he try to steal her attention. She...she has too much on her plate to worry about some fucker in Missouri. It's unacceptable, I can already tell he isn't good enough. I can...

Chill the fuck out man, she's pulling your chain.

"Yeah? Why?"

"Why what, Nadia?"

"Why do you have a problem with that? With Levi wanting to take me out and treat me like a lady."

"Because you're mine, don't you understand that. I'm not sure what p art of that you've missed but I'll be damned if some pansy who couldn't protect his DVD player takes you on a shit-ass candle lit dinner date. Besides, he's such a square, if he knows anything about you he'd realize that his lame fucking dates will have you dying of boredom."

Nadia leans over me at the end of my tirade. Her soft hands grazing my bare chest seconds before those sharp fucking nails of hers dig into my pecs, and the tips of her long hair tickle my heated skin. My brain takes a trip to the moon, cueing the dial-up tone and slow buffering, when she grinds her hips on me.

Kill me now.

"And what am I?"

"You...I..." She rocks again and I groan. *Unfair devil.* "fuck."

"What was that? I didn't catch it, Kaleb. I'm going to need you to speak up."

My hands snap to her hips and grip them to the point the contours of her hipbones fight against the force. She tries to roll again, but I control it; muscles in my chest and biceps straining to contain my unraveling sanity.

"You're...you're like me, sweetheart. Adrenaline. Danger. That's what you are. Craving fear and arousal in one shot of high octane. Typical dates would drive you mad, have you running for the hills just to escape the idea of sitting through another one."

Stilling, she lays on me again, where my heart beats harder than a war drum next to her more calm and steady thumps.

"Right you are. I like the unknown, things that might hurt me, get me in trouble, and that's what I'll have with you. Speed, envious stares, all because I won the bad boy."

Capturing her lips, we kiss for God knows how long. Forgetting about any and everything that exists outside of our bubble–the only thing that matters is us, but time's ticking away. We've been here for a few hours it seems. The moon has been in the sky so long it's also getting tired, easing its way closer to the horizon. Breaking the kiss, I peek at the radio and see three am blinking at me. Immediately I want to roll it back, find some sort of science project that allows me to time travel back far enough to relive today over again.

Dropping my head to the seat, I sigh. It's time to go back, for me to let her go for just a few days. Which gives me the chance to race and get the boxes she may need to move—between you and I, she doesn't need anything from her childhood home but if she wants to bring something with her I want to be prepared.

Ten more minutes, I can do this for ten more. Map every curve and dip of her body, the freckles I've noticed scattered over her shoulders and the larger more-sparse ones over her back. Taste her lips a bit longer, draw in breaths from my favorite damn person imaginable, isolate every fragrance note in her body spray, and lose count of how many lashes she has only to start again.

"Wasn't ever a competition, sweetheart. You've always had me," I murmur under my breath.

Time is up before I realize it, I have to get her back to the truck and home before asshat figures out she's been gone all night. I think I may even follow her home–we'll chalk it up to being safe.

Instead of saying we need to leave, knowing the words will feel like barbed wire and razors coming up my throat, I dress her instead. This is the least she deserves–to be doted on and worshiped, cared for in a way that's foreign to both of us but feels more right than wrong. On a selfish level? It gives me more opportunity to touch her since I have so much time to make up for.

Once she's put back together, I rush into my jeans and shirt, not bothering with zipping up or with my belt.

"Ready to go back? Your friends are probably wondering where you're at and mine are likely face down in the dirt, drunk."

"Not really."

It breaks my heart hearing the sadness in her voice. There's nothing that will make it better and I hate it, she deserves so much more. It's eating me alive knowing she will have to exist in her feelings for the next few days, but then everything will change–I promise. There won't be any more days where she shuts herself away in her room, and now that she's done with school and willing to leave with me, she never has to hide again.

People can't live like that, shut off from those who care the most about them or the world for that matter. Humans are social creatures, we need community and companionship to survive. What she has in that house is anything but survival at the hands of the man she calls father. Imagine having friends but still being lonely, how isolated that feels, solitary without the bars and caged windows that come along with it. It will kill her—diminish what light she has left inside, when all I ever want is to turn up the heat and set the world on fire for her. Maybe that's the reason behind the firebug living in her heart; it's her way of letting her light shine and be as destructive as she needs to just keep herself from being swallowed by self-pity and depression.

Hitting the ignition, the car starts with ease, *Cinderella* coming through to sideswipe us with a slow and sad tempo. I want to change it, to move it away from the heartache pouring out of the speakers but I don't because it encompasses all that's left of our time together. I know exactly what I have and I'm going to hold on to it for dear life if it's the last thing I do.

Shifting into drive, we creep up the gravel road back to the main route in relative silence–heavy, suffocating, silence. The blacktop pulls the rubber tires onto the dark, dew-covered surface like a magnet, then we're off weaving through the backroads once more. Dread settles deep into the pit of both our stomachs with every mile we eat up and there's not a damn thing I can do to stop it.

Finally on the main highway, Nadia fills my right peripheral, being there just isn't enough. When we hit a straightaway, I shift and look at her profile. She seems too tired for a woman her age, as if life has already sucked all of the youth out of her and she's waiting for the inevitable end for her, and her pain both. I promise to never add to it, to only ever lift her up even if I have to drag her with me.

Parting my lips, so I may tell her I love her again, red and blue lights explode behind us. High beams and a spotlight pierce the near-black interior of the cab–borderline blinding me for several blinks.

Nadia tries to look over her shoulder, her fair complexion catching the purple blend of flashing reds and blues. I don't slow down but don't speed up either, waiting for her command. If she wants me to stop then I will and we can go sit in lockup together until arraignment, but I have a feeling she won't.

Sirens join in with the robotic order to pull over that sends goosebumps down my arms and my heart into overdrive. The officer shouts another grating warning through the megaphone attached to the cruiser's front bumper.

Come on, Diabolica. Tell me if we're running or not.

"Nadia..."

There's a pause, a split second between the wailing siren and our breaths that has me on the edge of my damn seat. One that's entirely too long but finally, finally, her decision comes.

"Lose 'em." For the second time tonight, she said something similar. Dare I hope this will become routine? If so, I love it.

"With pleasure."

Slamming my foot to the clutch, it's down for a split moment before my hand shifts the Civic into a lower gear. Transitioning from clutching to the gas pedal, the torque of the car slows us then everything changes when we rocket off. RPM's reach the red zone again and again, through every shift, before the gears slide into sixth and the officer loses ground.

The straight shot we're on bends into the curve of the mountains closer we get to Hazelwood, yet the officer hasn't given up which makes me think he's not city or even county, he's a state fucking trooper–more trouble than any of us can afford. My NOS is spent too, fuck we don't have a means to get away unless something else happens. If we keep doing this—running—there will be a helicopter in the air and warrants for the both of us before mornings end.

"Kaleb...what do we do?" Nadia asks, fear saturating her worry.

Retrieving my phone from my pocket, I go through the contacts quickly and press it to my ear—knowing just the asshole to call. One ring, two rings, silence, then relief hits when his voice comes through.

"Reeeeyyyy, my man. Where'd you go? This party is boring as fuuuuck."

"Fuentes, I need a favor."

"That so? You have the means to pay me?"

"Not really but it will be a good time either way."

"I'm listening."

The officer flashes his lights, giving me my final warning before he pulls out his next trick, I mean I think that's what it is but I'm not going to second guess myself.

"I'm on the highway with company and out of NOS. Think you can give him something better to chase?"

He won't say no, not when there's an opportunity to show the law how he is untouchable nor the chance to smoke me in a race. While this won't be one, so to speak, he'll be our saving grace and pull the officer's attention in a different direction. I wait, and wait, and wait, hearing noise on his side of the phone fade then the thud of his car door—relief washing through me.

"How far out are you?"

"Ten miles east."

"See you in five."

As quickly as he answered the phone, he hung up, the line dying, my phone lighting up the side of my face. Dropping the damn thing into the cup holder, I look over at Nadia and see she's caught on.

"You called in a distraction?"

Smart girl.

"Yes ma'am. You ready for this?"

"Fuck...I hope so."

The pedal is on the floor, the officer no longer flashing his lights, and barely keeps up for miles, then I see it. Those stupid fucking running lights Fuentes has on Bitch Maker and...

"Kaleb..." Nadia's voice tightens when she sees what I do.

"Fuck!"

The asshole is running up the wrong side of the damn highway! Heading straight for us at breakneck speeds, whipping by what few cars there are on the road.

"KALEB!"

Chapter Eleven

Nadia's cry for me has my heart stuttering—something's wrong, the tone and slight shake in the pitiful sound is all wrong. *She's terrified*. Glancing over, I see her struggling with her harness and son of a bitch! It's not on, one shoulder strap's hanging loose and twisted in the metal clasp as she desperately tries to get the other buckled in time. It's unsafe, dangerous even, and not the type that either of us prefers. If we go off the road, it will kill her.

Shit!

Steadying the wheel as much as possible, I reach over and swat her fighting hands away. I don't give a fuck if the straps are twisted in the buckles, it needs to be tightened; right now. Especially with Fuentes's crazy ass leading us into the possibility of a head-to-head collision. Not only that but we're in the fucking country and though I haven't concerned myself with it until now, there's no telling if something will jump out in front of us before the maniac makes it here.

This is going to hell real fucking fast, true fear is taking root and I don't know what to do to ease it. Outside of the trooper and Fuentes, if more first responders appear we're done for. What the fuck happens if we crash and she's ejected? Zap and I planned for it but it's not enough when you're staring the possibility in the face. That's why we installed these damn harnesses but hers, it's failing her. I can't, no, I absolutely will not lose control right now. It's not an option when I have invaluable cargo.

With her hands out of the way, I grab the strap's tongue and yank with all of my strength. Stupid thing refuses to budge at first, then I yank again. My muscles burn from my shoulder down to my mechanic's grip the longer I hold on and force the strap through the tight metal binding. The car swerves when it gives way, cinching down across her hips, and my body jerks to the side.

Both hands back on the steering wheel, they white knuckled the hard circle as Fuentes quickly approaches. This part of the highway is two-lane but moving at these speeds, and banked with trees on both sides, it's going to be a breath holding-tight fit.

Two miles away.

One mile away.

His lights die out, killing half of the brightness between our cars, taking the brunt of the blindness as Nadia and I hold our breaths. The seconds tick by in painfully slow increments; inches disappear in still shots rather than motion. It's said you relive the greatest moments of your life in the last seven minutes of brain activity—this is not that. This is a train wreck happening in real time and I can't look away; absolutely zero self-preservation.

In a flash, time fast forwards—I see Fuentes's stupid fucking face as our cars squeeze by one another with a cartoonish like stretch, followed by the blur of his running lights streaking through the left side of my vision.

Snapping my eyes to the rearview, I see the officer drastically slow down, distance and the night's darkness devouring what's left of his headlights. I can't look for long, the road is moving too damn fast for me to be distracted for too long—she keeps watching the encounter behind us though, taking note of the ballsy move Fuentes made.

She lets out a sigh, turning back in her seat once the red and blues finally race after Fuentes instead–asshole will be on me for that favor before I know it. Actually, I give him twenty-four hours before he's hitting my phone and needing me for some sort of ride along.

Between him and Emmett, I'm going to end up in jail–something I'm sure Uncle impatiently waiting for. He'll use the time to make an example out of me. What not to do in our family, how not to embarrass my Ma, etcetera. If anyone is going to show up in the headlines as a disgrace, it will be him. How? I don't know, but I know it's coming and believe me, I look forward to the day.

Focused, my hands hold the wheel at ten and two, we're both doing our best to come down without an adrenaline crash. Surprisingly, a giddy laugh at my right startles me. Nadia's head is leaned back against the headrest, and she's fucking losing it. Heavy breaths expand and deflate from her chest when she gasps only to keep laughing. That's it, she's gone completely insane.

I mean, I know we have been on multiple adrenaline highs tonight but she's at her crashing point, frankly, so am I. The moment she gets home, and crawls into her too-small bed, she's going to pass out. For how long, who knows, but I won't be shocked if it's for a good ten to twelve hours like she's just come off of a forty-eight-hour acid trip. She deserves it though.

Of everything I've put her through tonight, her falling asleep in the safety of her bed is the least of my concerns.

"What's so funny, sweetheart?"

"I...I don't know. I just need to laugh. It's...it's so much."

"Tell me about it."

Alone on the highway once again, the off ramp for Hazelwood comes up quickly; a single self-serve gas station sits at the very end for people to use at all times of the night. Hitting the blinker, it clicks softly with Nadia's residual giggles. The orange flicker reflecting off cars parked in a mom-and-pop car dealership next door, as well as the barred station windows.

Guiding the Civic off the highway, I ease on the brake, slowing down just in time to pull into the lot illuminated by one lonely light.

My nerves are slowing down, either that, or the rest of my body is finally catching up now that I'm done outrunning my guardian angels. At a pump, I shift the car into park and climb out to fuel up. The numbers on the pump roll by slowly, one right after another, while I wait with my hands tucked into my pockets–a little chilly outside for a late spring, early summer, night.

Nadia's door opens, pulling my attention away from the pump when her toe pressing to the filthy concrete. It's not quite open all of the way, but it hasn't caught wind or flung open either, simply resting on the back of her calf while she moves around. Curiously, I watch rather than intervene or ask her what she's doing–I like to be surprised sometimes, so why not be patient this once.

When I hear the radio station switch and the volume increase, I turn back to the pump and pray to the heavens–she's going to ruin me. A fucking piano and acoustic guitar maintain a slow melody when she pushes the door wide and joins me. I can't resist her when she reaches for me. Vacating my jacket pocket, my hand takes hers and spins her around with her hand high above her head. John Michael Montgomery's singing about Cinderella and Prince Charming, moving heaven and earth, giving everything he has to the woman he loves and the weight of his devotion resonates deep in my heart.

Pulling her into my arms, seeing her face full of so much happiness and those beautiful eyes staring up at me in awe, I finally recognized it. She's here with me, truly, in the moment and though she doesn't express her feelings the same way I do, I can read the devotion written in every micro-expression. The world may be blind, but I'm not, not while we dance right here at the damn pump.

Nadia doesn't move how I imagined she would; like we're at prom, both nervous and stiff. No, she has one hand on my chest, the other slid around to my back where she's holding onto me as fervently as I'm holding her. Dipping an arm around her waist, the other braces her delicate jawline, my fingers teasing into her hair, and a thumb caresses her cheek.

I'm not a singer, so I'm not going to punish her with my tone-deaf drawl, but that's not stopping me from kissing her. Hoping, praying, knowing she feels just how in love I am with her at this very moment–if she wants heaven and earth, she can have it. My heart, sold. However she wants to be loved, it's hers.

Just take it, please. Hold it in your hands, sweetheart. Keep it warm and safe, but whatever you do, never let it go.

Breaking the kiss, our foreheads press together when *Bad Company* queues up next—a bit more my speed but I'm not complaining. I'll stand here until the sun breaks the sky and the world wakes up in a frenzy just to keep dancing with her as if nothing else exists.

Breaking the spell, the rude as hell gas pump shuts off with a loud thump.

"This has been the best night of my life, Nadia." I can't bring myself to talk normally, a whisper is all she gets. I don't want this to end–still wishing for that time travel device knowing it will never come, but if it did, I would turn back to the moment she took my breath away at the bonfire. Then I would do it a hundred times more, repeating our greatest hits.

"Mine too, Rey. Thank you for tonight. You scared me and had me worried in all the wrong ways, just to turn around and give me a graduation night I could have only dreamed about."

"Don't have to thank me, I want you to have everything you've ever wanted. Especially if I'm the one who ends up in your arms at the end of the night. Pretty fair trade if you ask me."

Kissing her again, I hug her tight to me and rest my chin on the top of her head. Both content in standing here taking up space and time—whatever it takes to keep from returning her to her stupid friends and her dick of a dad. These next few days are going to be the longest ones of my life, especially after having her all to myself with nothing else in the way.

Reluctantly, I help her back to her seat, buckle her harness, and shut the door. Finishing up at the gas pump I make my way around the back of the car then fold myself into the driver seat; unapologetically bummed now we're officially out of time. It's almost five in the morning, her dad will be looking for her, likely on a rampage since she never let him know she would be out until the ass-crack of dawn–fingers crossed he hasn't been drinking or doing some other equally mind-altering substance.

"Ready?"

Poor thing's getting tired, she's slightly slumped in her seat and leaning back a bit more than she was earlier. "Mhm."

Leaving the gas station in the dust, we're back on the road and about five minutes from the bonfire. On our way we pass a few students I recall seeing at the gathering before Nadia showed up and we took off. Fingers crossed they make it home safely and without having a run in with the cops—though most of the police don't give a shit in Hazelwood. They're too busy flirting at the diner or sitting on the outskirts popping people in speed traps.

Finally, the trees framing the road open up to the field with still several cars remaining and a more relaxed-looking atmosphere. Of course my boys are here still, patiently waiting for me to scoop them up. Her friends, unsurprisingly, are loitering too–fuckers can't do a damn thing without Nadia needing to be present. I was honestly impressed to see them here before she arrived, they took initiative and didn't need her to hold their fucking hands; they're growing up, I'm so proud.

Eyeroll.

I hate them. The longer I'm with her, the more I claim her, the less civil I will be when they come around to hang on her coattails . Yeah yeah, I know, I shouldn't judge them or make her choose and the truth is I won't; but she'll do it when she finally learns she's out of their league. Ivy is the absolute worst, she's going to be a terrible influence on her one day—or leave her high and dry when she needs her the most. I can't wait, anything to get rid of that trifling bitch.

Though people have filtered out, there are still more here than I thought there would be at give in the morning. At least the fire has died down and it looks like the fire department didn't show up either with how dry the ground is.

"Oh sweet, my friends are still here." Nadia chimes in, plucking me from my thoughts.

"Lucky them." I say dryly. "Sorry, I didn't..."

"Yes you did. You don't have to hide it, Rey. I know you don't like them. They're all I have though."

"That's not true, and you know it."

Lord give me strength. I don't want to end tonight with a disagreement. Let me just keep my mouth shut and crawl this car along the uneven pasture. No, no I'm not leaving things between us like this; fuck that.

"You have me, Nadia. I know that's only one more person in your corner, but it's still one more. I'll always be here fighting for you. Tell me...tell me you believe me."

Parking in an empty space close to where I parked earlier I see another vehicle come in behind us that swings over by her truck. Nadia virtually leaps out of the car before I get it in park but she's not faster than me. Reaching for her, I snag her shirt, and pull her back inside.

"Sweetheart, talk to me."

"I don't want to talk anymore, Rey. I want to go home."

"Do you believe me?" I ask again, not letting her go.

She won't look me in the eye and I'm not having any of that shit. This behavior comes from how her dad treats her. When things get a little too uncomfortable, she shuts down and it's like trying to break into Fort Knox. I won't allow it, we're going to learn healthier ways to communicate after tonight. Our relationship deserves that much.

Leaning, I hook a finger under her chin and turn her to me, my free hand circling around to the back of her head, cradling so she can't look away from me. There's sadness there. The untamed laughter from earlier long gone, leaving the emotional fallout of having to leave. I steal the softest peck from her lips, the bottom one beginning to tremble. She doesn't want to talk because that means speaking on her feelings and that prickly exterior is her own protection; she's hurting I know this, and too damn proud to cry.

"I'm coming back for you. Whether you believe me or not. I may not be able to convince you now, that I'm yours and you're mine, but I will. Give me a few days, okay? When your dad leaves for work on Monday, I'll be there to get you. Do you understand?"

Silence—the kind that's so damn loud it's deafening. Pressing one last kiss to her forehead, I release her.

"Come on, let's get out there. I'll stay until you head home."

Out of the car, the doors close with a thud as her vulture-esque friends swarming her as mine approach me from the opposite side. We bump knuckles, Wes flies into something completely unrelated, failing to capture my interest. Zap's at my side, his arms crossed over his chest watching me watch her.

"You going to be able to leave when she does, Rey?" He asks under the cover of Wes's stupid story.

"Don't have a choice man. We have shit to do and she has to go home. Pretend everything's okay and that she's not going to up and disappear on Monday."

"Does that mean she agreed? That's good news, man. I can't wait to get to know her and see her around on campus. Will be nice to have someone else to talk to other than Wes. Are you still planning on staying in the dorms, or are you going to try and get your own place?"

"Will definitely find our own space as soon as possible. I don't want her around Wes—fucker is a pig. Then I can have her all to myself without putting up with you two, no offense."

"None taken. You're a good guy, Rey. I'm glad she's choosing you over all of this. You deserve to be happy and I'm sure she does too."

Ivy is fawning all over Nadia right now, drunk off her ass and hanging on her like a wet blanket. Not a good look if you ask me but good thing she never was on my radar despite being on hers. She sets off all sorts of warning bells in my head, the other two aren't as bad but still. From the looks of it, Zap hasn't given her any attention either; he's got a foul look on his face as he glances at her. Thank God. Dodged a bullet with that one.

"Girl, you missed it. Oh my god. They were out here doing keg stands, passing joints around. It was like that frat party I snuck out to with Oliver!" Ivy hiccups at the end.

"Dammit, Ivy, that was a secret!"

"It's alright, Oli, not really my scene anyway." Nadia responds politely then shoves Ivy off of her, returning to me. Wes and Zap step aside, knowing she is my top priority and forever will be.

"I believe you," she whispers.

My heart, it's going to burst. My whole life is standing in front of me, making a promise without meaning to with those three little inconspicuous words.

A couple of car doors slam shut, a few more of the lightweights heading home for the day. When her friends suddenly learn how to shut up and go silent, unease settles over me. I can't stomach what's unfolding, hearing the worst voice we could have imagined screaming her name from nowhere.

My eyes snap to the furious man stalking over, he's on a rampage, his face a deep shade of red and eyes as black as coal.

The second we realize what's about to happen, we both freeze.

CHAPTER TWELVE

"Nadia Rayle Pierce!"

Nadia whips around like someone just screamed her from the fucking grave, then she turns a few shades lighter than I have seen her all night. A wave of fear drapes over her; stifling and erasing every bit of happiness she managed to bottle up tonight.

"Fuck, it's my dad."

There's no doubt about it, he remembers me by the way he glares at me with unbridled disgust. We've passed each other a time or two and I'll never tell Nadia but he's delivered some not-so-nice words in the past. I've never been afraid of him and if it ever came down to it he would be on his ass before he had the chance to spit another vile insult. He's since kept his temper in check around me but it seems that he's become bold in my absence.

Actively choosing to keep my cool, the leather of my jacket creeks when my arms cross defensively over my chest and I lean against the hood of Delinquent. My ankles repeat a similar process right as Gene's eyes shift from Nadia to me. Venom encrusted daggers shoot in my direction as he glowers, the possession in them wills me to disintegrate where I stand. He can scowl at me all he wants, it's not going to prevent me from having anything to do with his daughter.

Boy, are you in for one hell of a surprise—asshole.

"I've been looking everywhere for you. Get your ass in the goddamn truck. We are going home!" Gene shouts.

"Alright, alright!" Her voice pierces the atmosphere, drawing more glances from the embarrassed yet too nosey for their own good classmates.

"Don't you fuckin' raise your voice at me, Nadia. I'll beat that attitude right out of your smart fucking mouth."

Red.

Pure, raging, blood-red, fills my vision. He grabs her arm then yanks her forward, putting too much distance between her and I. That's all it takes to haul me away from the car and back onto my boots.

Who the hell does this mother fucker think he is? Putting his hands on her and threatening her like she's goddamn property? She's an adult for fucks sake; capable of making her own decisions including turning her back on me if she feels the need to. That's her damn decision to make, one without him trying to puppet her into following his commands.

His selective concern grates every single raw nerve ending I have, stoking the fury in my gut, and I know the asshole can see it. He wants this, wants her to see how I react and show her the kind of man I can be under all the leather and soft words. If he wants her to see it, to watch me shed the layers I hide under because they remind me too much of uncle, then I will. I'll be whatever monster he's baiting me to be.

Following them in a storm of fury, my whole body unexpectedly comes to a halt when two forces meet both shoulders—Wes on my right, Zap on my left. They have their arms bound around me in some sort of hold I instinctively fight despite their snake-like grips. Every protective instinct I have flares to life when I hear Nadia yelp. Wrestling harder against them, my nostrils flare, aiding the wave or adrenaline that bursts into my blood stream.

This is worse than the highway, worse than running from the cops and doing work for Emmett. Seeing her stop and turn, scuffling with her dad's iron grip, I fight Wes and Zap harder. She's trying to get back to me, back to where she's safe–away from the one dousing her with fear. Nadia pushes at his fist, Converse staggering through vehicle-crushed grass and over hidden dips in the earth.

Jerking, my boys put all of their weight on me to prevent me from closing the distance, pissing me off even more. I'm absolutely ready to slam my fist into both of their faces if it means they release me so I can make it to her before her dad does something worse.

Painfully, the pull she has on me frays, the universe slowly tearing us apart from each other and it's gutting me—leaving a pit in my stomach. She must feel it too cause the second it snaps, her spine straightens and her mask slips over her face again. Shielding herself from a world designed to decimate all of her beauty.

Fuck, FUCK!

Shaking the guys off of me, I watch helplessly when she's thrown into the driver seat of the truck; Gene follows behind her, slamming the door so hard it rattles the vehicle's metal exterior. Counting the seconds between every one of my hurried steps, the truck comes alive before I can make it to the passenger door.

Red light spills across the field, telling me he's shifting the truck into drive; a breath later powerful headlights hit a few onlookers in the face, forcing them to shy away. There's too much silence, a story altering episode of our lives broadcasted for others to see. I hate it, I hate him for doing this to her, for showing people what goes on behind doors, for hurting her.

I don't know what to do, my angels are shouting for me to let her go while the demons inside want me to rip Gene limb from limb, then there's that stupid logical side telling me that there's nothing I can do right now. I can't fight a fucking truck, I can't pry the door open like I'm Superman trying to save the girl. I can't even shoot my way through this, not because that's not the type of man I am but I don't have the means to do so.

I'm at a total loss—emotionally, mentally, and now physically when the brake lights dim and the truck pulls away.

No, no no no no no.

"Nadia!"

Dirt kicks up into my face when Gene gives it more gas, pushing it faster and harder out of the field, and putting other bystanders in danger. Flexing my hands, waiting, watching as the taillights fade into the dark after he pulls onto the blacktop road and guns it.

I can't breathe, he's taken my whole world with him out of spite and ownership. The urge to run, scream, and threaten him within an inch of his life has wedged under my skin where the slightest movement or brush ignites in pain.

I have to keep it together–fuck Kaleb bring it in!

Chastising myself, I know this is only temporary and in a few days' time she will be back with me, escaping Gene and his control. She'll be happier–she promised to run away with me, to leave and never return to

Hazelwood and I'm going to hold her to that. A promise is a promise, so she has to do it. I just hope he doesn't do something so bad that it convinces her to stay here and forget about me.

Grabbing the bottom of my jacket and jerking, it straightens as my back does. There's a plan in place, I just have to wait a little longer and any amount of falling apart now isn't going to save her come Monday. It's the expectant eyes staring through me from every direction that's keeping me rooted. They're asking themselves why I didn't do more to help her—the disappointment and sadness poisoning the air so heavily I'm ready to buckle beneath it.

I don't want to leave this spot—the ground has a hold of me all over again where it subtly shifts under my boots, threatening to open up and swallow me deep into its belly out of shame. I don't want to leave her, or this night in the past. That thought alone is breaking me in half. This field, and this night if I'm being honest, will live in my mind as both a blessing and a curse.

"Rey..." Zap's voice comes from behind me, barely loud enough for anyone to hear other than me. I know what he's doing, attempting to ground me, bring me back to a more levelheaded place so I can function like a normal fucking man. The need is there, trying so hard to cocoon me in its protective embrace but it's not enough. I need more, I need—her.

"Rey." Wes calls out next, his hand wrapping around my elbow just like Gene had grabbed Nadia. Yanking away from him, my fists bunch the front of his shirt and shove him back until we find something more solid to stand against—someone's SUV. Nose to nose, if looks could kill he'd be dead where he stands. This shit isn't his fault, he's never done anything to me other than piss me off because he wants to be a pest. Right now though, all of my anger is aimed squarely at him. I'm about to break something of his when Zap tries to squeeze between us.

"Rey, man. Stop, he isn't the one. I know, I know you're torn up. We know you can't help it but fuck...don't hit him." Wes is silent, watching me work through the whole ordeal without egging me into a fight he will lose. He knows I don't mean it, but part of me can't decipher logic—can't separate my anger from my heartache.

"Come on, Rey, let him go. It's okay." Zap's voice softens. Doing what he can to bring me away from throwing myself off that proverbial cliff, the one I'd willingly fall over if it meant saving Nadia.

Time is nothing, it's ticking by in agonizing seconds; one right after the other that almost feels like nothing. Warm and firm hands ease my grip open, it's a feat at first, but they finally loosen and fall to my sides. Relief and guilt both swarm me, simultaneously sharp and soothing.

"I'm sorry," I say. Stepping back from Wes, lightly brushing his shirt and shoulders off in the only way I can show my remorse. He's a shithead, yeah, but he didn't deserve me doing that to him.

"Don't apologize, man. I know you're going through it. Let us help you."

Help—I huff. That's all they've done for me is help. Since day one, the moment I walked out of my ma's house and left for college he's helped me. This day has been a long time in the making, his unusual assistance supporting me while I played chess with my life. Manipulating every decision, taking Nadia into consideration with each so our lives perfectly aligned when she was ready. It's not fair to them.

We planned for this, for her dad to find out or show up at some point—now or ten years down the road. Playing his fucking games, aiming to control every aspect of her life, emotionally and mentally wreck her all for his own personal gain. The problem lies in my inability to keep calm. I tried, I really did, water off the back. I tried feigning nonchalance, so Gene wouldn't knife himself under my skin and lodge deep into my heart by taking Nadia away, but he did anyway.

I thought I was prepared for this but now I know I'm not—it's going to take much more to keep my head above water now that we have seen how well I hold my composure. Zap and Wes are needed now more than ever—they're the support system I have, might not be the only one I've got, but they're here. Ma would have my back. She fucking loves Nadia nearly as much as I do, and if going to bat for my girl was what it took, my mom would be next to me with her chancla, ready to protect Nadia. Much can't be said for her shitty-ass friends who did nothing but stand by and watch.

As a matter of fact...

Wrenching heavily to the left, I see the three of them huddling next to Ivy's car. She's filing her nails while Wren chews hers and Oliver fiddles with an MP3 player. Worthless, absolutely pointless, selfish, humans.

What fizzling rage remained bursts into another wrath filled shit-storm. Crossing the open space, I'm standing before Ivy before my brain can catch up, slapping her nail file out of her hand. Oliver looks up, Wren ceases her anxious chewing, but Ivy? The bitch says nothing, those slowly-dying eyes of hers meet mine and I see it.

"You called him." Not a question, or accusation, a revelation. This frigid whore is so jealous of Nadia she willingly sabotaged someone who she supposedly cares for. Someone who's protected all three of them in the past, now she stares at me unapologetically as her imps hang off her like skin tags when she speaks up.

"I don't know what you're talking about."

"Bullshit, Ivy! You called Gene and told him where Nadia was."

Puzzle pieces snap loudly into place. How long we've been gone, how we've been here for maybe five minutes before Gene showed up—then it dawns on me, he followed us into the field. Ivy wanted him to see us together and when Nadia climbed out of my car, he got the confirmation he needed.

"Think you're clever, don't you?" I accuse, closing the space where she can barely see anyone past me and I'm filling every one of her fucking senses. Threatening, boding, and ready to choke the life out of her.

"Do you think this is how you win me, Ivy? I've seen you flutter those clumpy eyelashes at me, twirl your fake-ass blonde hair around your finger, in hopes I'll notice you. Truth is, I have. You've hovered in my peripherals for years like an annoying gnat that's just slightly too fast for me to kill."

She straightens, her face turning red but she doesn't look away, confident in her silence and aware her peons have no control or say in this situation. If it comes to my boys versus them, I'll drag Ivy across this field and fling her cold body into a ditch for what she's done.

Leaning in, my breath and barely contained disgust whisper next to her fake-diamond pierced ear.

"It will never be you."

Ivy goes to speak but I catch her by the throat and shove her back against the car, forcing the air from her lungs. Squeezing her airway to show her exactly how it feels to have someone she thought was safe hold her life in their hands.

"This is what's going to happen, so listen closely you fucking shrew. You and your so-called groupies are going to fade out of Nadia's life. It will start small, missed messages, forgetting to return calls—you'll make it look like you all got too busy with your lives. Then after a few years you'll disappear in one way or another—by accident, by force... it doesn't matter to me."

I can't help but squeeze her throat tighter when she squirms, the weight of her hands finding my chest to push when she discovers oxygen depletes quickly. She fights harder, expending her energy with the same level of fear I witnessed in Nadia's eyes flaring in her own. Still, I hold on. I'm not above choking her the hell out and letting the dogs here rough her up if they want to. She deserves to taste this, to see what not having control looks like.

"You don't deserve Nadia, she's too good for you. She's smart, engaging, she sets me on fire in ways you never would have. Nadia caged my heart next to hers which makes you fucking invisible. You are nothing to me and will be nothing to her in the end—mark my words, Ivy. There will come a day where you're as dead to Nadia as you are to me."

Shoving her away, I use her neck as the foundation of the force, cracking the back of her head against the window with a low hollow thud. Ivy gasps, Oliver and Wren rush to her side to render aid, but I don't give a flying fuck. Fuck her, fuck them. They will all get what's coming to them and I'll sell my fucking soul to make sure it happens.

Have you ever been so angry you feel your cells vibrating? Or completely numb to your surroundings you practically forget where you're currently existing and need to run off of autopilot? That's exactly where I'm at. Logical thinking is nonexistent while standing here, the laid back and softer side of me has taken the backseat in my head while my violence shifts through the motions.

"Let's go." I announce. Zap and Wes don't argue, they don't make a peep when we climb into Delinquent and leave this sorry excuse for a party.

There are only two things in this world right now that will calm me down and one is probably climbing into her bed and crying her eyes out. The other is the road. Rubber on pavement, the smell of rich-burning fuel, and a checkered flag at the end of a finish line.

The guys hold on as I take my anger out on the drive, whipping deep into the bend of curves and flying through empty four-way stop signs. It's still too early for anyone to be out on a Saturday morning, which I'm thankful for, makes it easier getting to Wes's parents where I can drop them off.

I need to be alone, to cycle through every overwhelming emotion that refuses to release me and the sooner I can get there, the better.

Pulling up to the house, they step out and shut the door. Zap leans over, placing his hands on the window seal trying to give me some bullshit words of encouragement that fall on deaf ears.

"Go home and clear your head, man. You have a race today. I know you're eating yourself alive right now but you can't be like this come Monday. Nadia's going to need you as a whole man, not a pissed off one."

"Fuck off." I bite back.

"Gladly, but seriously. Go home and see your ma. We will see you later. Love you, man."

"Love you too."

Not the manliest response but I do, I love him. He's such a good dude. None of us should be dealing with the shit that we are but he has a kid to think about, not my ass. Leaning over, we bump knuckles then I'm pulling off again. My mom will be up, expecting me to already be in bed and waking up to her homemade breakfast when the delicious scents waft through the trailer.

As soon as I pull up, I see her peeking out of the kitchen window and catch her brows furrowing. Part of me can't move from where I was with Nadia last, but I know keeping my mom waiting isn't going to speed up time. The shower is calling my name, along with a full plate of breakfast, and my bed. I need to relax, rest, and get ready for the race I've waited months for.

When I step inside, the door shuts behind me as I start moving through the motions of toeing off my boots and shrugging out of my jacket. Chorizo is sizzling along with bacon which assaults my senses—my stomach grumbles with hunger for the inviting aroma. I miss being here, coming home to someone who thinks I've hung the moon and then some of the stars.

Bootless, I move through the small living room with hand me down sofas and a coffee table with one leg slightly too short, then into the kitchen right as she sets down my plate with the tell-tale clank of the ceramic. I stop, looking at the food then over to her, my rock and strength wrapped in one loving package.

Within seconds, I fall apart. She rushes to me and pulls me down to her shorter height, hugging me tight to shush my tears.

"I know, mi hijo. I know."

CHAPTER THIRTEEN

Festering—like the sour scent of old fuel and years of burnt motor oil. That's the only way I can explain the past sixteen hours. I took my shower after scarfing down mom's food that lost its flavor between my breakdown and stepping under the spray. Sleeping was a fool's errand, I tossed and turned, replaying the entire night in my mind. Emmett and the job, the police chase, Fuentes, Gene, Ivy—it's all so fucking heavy.

When I woke up around eleven, I got dressed and left. There was nowhere else to go, or things to do. I needed the fresh air and let go of what wasn't currently serving me. I'm not blaming Nadia by any means but the shit that always seems to follow her around is draining without my own to add to it. There's no understanding how tiresome this life has been for her and what's worse is there are people who have lived through more unimaginable things.

While I've never been super religious, despite coming from a Catholic background, I can't help but ask the age old question of 'why'. Why do bad things happen to good people? Why does the church continue to say God gives his hardest struggles to his strongest soldiers? It's ass backwards–give the hard shit to the bad apples. Why does he continue to torment the people who only want to live their lives in peace and just be? All it's doing is setting them up for failure—depression, anxiety, ideation—and that's heartbreaking enough.

I'm angry, bone deep, soul shaking, angry, and I have no idea how to cope with it. Other than a few hiccups in my early years, I was never taught how to deal with these types of emotions. Love and appreciation are completely different—my mom made sure I was mature in that sense. She raised me into being a man who would value vulnerability, yet with all her love and support, anger management wasn't on the curriculum. That would have been something I learned from my old man but that's not a story I want to tell.

All I have is Uncle Ren who leads with hatred and narcissism which is the reason we fight—we are opposites and volatile. The last thing I want to do is heed words of advice from a man who detests his own family and heritage.

The plan for today is to get the car ready: tire rotation, air check, NOS replenish, system checks, safety inspections, equipment inventory, the full gauntlet. She needs to be in tip top shape for this race, I have an impression to make and a career to bag before leaving this shit hole with my girl.

Tucked away in the garage at Wes's parents, the hood is up with Zap under it, his computer plugged into the modules looking for any bugs or odd codes the car may be throwing. At the back, Wes is finishing up with the tires while I roll the NOS canister on its edge across the concrete slab floor. Once he squeezes out from under the back, he eases the jack down and pulls it free from the frame, the metal wheels creaking and clanking from too many years of being pinned between thousands of pounds and the unforgiving ground.

The Doors are whining in the background, pouring through speakers with the ambient sound of rain on the same track–*Riders on the Storm*–it's almost fitting but it keeps me in the zone; averting my impending spiral into the abyss of anger. This is the shit I can drive to late at night when it's just me and my thoughts. There are a few other tracks that have a similar effect on me and I plan to hunt for them on the radio when I finish up with the race and take my victory drive.

Listen to me, getting ahead of myself. That's alright, I'm ready for this. I've been training and burning through all of my finances to make sure that when I compete, Delinquent and I show up loud and perform perfectly. *Today is the day*. I'm landing a sponsorship before the end of the night, I've even conceded to attending church with my ma, then Monday I'm seeing Nadia again. It's all falling perfectly into place and I couldn't be happier—if it wasn't for the anger crawling beneath my skin, which reminds me...

"Hey, y'all finish up with what you're working on and let's grab a burger before we have to head to the track."

"Fucking hell, thought you'd never ask." Wes groans, immediately putting his tools away and wiping his hands off on a red grease rag. He's at the sink scooping a glob of Mean Green hand scrub onto his palm, quickly scrubbing it up to his elbows. "I've been thinking about that place right outside of town for days. They have this double bacon burger with a fried egg and hash browns on top. Best of both worlds if you ask me, breakfast and lunch in one go."

"That does sound good." Zap adds his two cents, setting his laptop aside then shutting the hood with a hard thump. "She's good to go, Rey. Tune up completed, all codes have been assessed and fixed. Did you get the NOS loaded?"

"Finishing up right now." I answer, screwing the refill hose to the connection. Twisting the valve on my canister, I switch to the other, twist the red crank and listen. The low hiss becomes much louder when one of them shuts off the radio and grabs their things. There's not much left to do other than drive and get a feel for the dynamics again—which won't take a lot since Delinquent is an extension of myself. I know her from inside and out. I can sense when something isn't quite right, when a lug nut's too loose, the RPM's shoot up too high too fast, even when the air conditioning is taking too long to cool down. She is me and I am her, we are a singular unit; a fast as hell, mean ass one at that.

Once the reservoir is full, I detach the canister and roll it back to the storage space, chaining it into place to keep it from getting knocked around or damaged. Grabbing my tool bag, it's loaded into the basket I keep bolted down in the trunk where Nadia got the turpentine from.

I drop into the driver seat, immediately melting. This is my pilot's chair, my throne, my favorite recliner I'm ready to fall asleep in at the end of a hard day's work. Reverently, I run my hands over the steering wheel, the hard leather smooth under my calloused grip.

I'm ready, we're ready.

Cranking the car, she hums loud in the garage. Music blasts, delivering bass directly to my sternum vibrating and warring for dominance over the pattering of my heart. Shifting her into gear, she crawls out of the open door and down the driveway where her rumble intensifies off the trees lining both sides of the outlet.

"She sounds fucking amazing, what did you do to her?"

"Tweaked the idle and exhaust output. Thought you might like it." Zap replies, shifting in his seat as I praise his work—guy has a kink he refuses to talk about.

"That slight pull to the right is gone too, Wes. Appreciate it."

"No problem man. She had some slight pressure differences and needed a quick balance but she's good to go, shouldn't experience any issues on the track," he replies.

I can't wait to open her up, feel the power she holds beneath us; we're going to be glorious on the track. Pulling onto the main road of the neighborhood, middle-class cars sit on both sides of the road as kids play in the front yards we drive by. Some of them look up then return back to their innocent play while others watch as we roll by. Those kids? They will remember this day, they will grow up and build model toy cars that look like mine. Then the ones they have tucked away in their toy boxes will get to drive across every surface in their home—all while dreaming of having their own life changing race one day. I hope they get it.

Fifteen minutes later Wes crowds Zap on their side of the booth, nudging each other's elbows trying to gain more table space. Fuckers already know what they want, but I keep coming back to the steak burger. It's got extra cheese and two patties with added sausage, slathered with miracle whip, mustard, pickles, onions, and dripping with grease. On the side sits a huge mound of shoestring fries, cooked to perfection, crispy outside and soft inside, salted the way I like them, and a big bowl of ranch to dip them into.

Between bites, I tend to a few texts on my phone. One says I'm almost about to run out of text-minutes which I ignore, others are quick good luck messages, and one where I'm conducting business. Emmett has been blowing me up all day, asking for another distraction, but I'm too busy to worry. He slips a question about Nadia in there and I force myself to ignore it. I told him what I needed and if this partnership is ever going to unfold, then he will need to follow through—I've done my good faith, it's his turn. One can only hope he doesn't blow me off.

"Bro, move the fuck over with your bony-ass elbows!" Wes bites out, Zap nearly hooks him in the face with it instead of moving. "I'm trying to eat here."

"I wouldn't have to push you if you wouldn't eat like a rabid dog. Slow down and chew, damn Hoover vacuum."

We all chuckle at that, sometimes he has good comebacks, other times it's as awkward as a baby giraffe trying to run. I smirk, both of my elbows braced comfortably on the table with all the free room in the world to move around, as I point a ranch coated fry at Wes.

"He has a point, should slow down before you choke on something. Unless you've managed to improve your gag reflexes when you were in jail."

"You're not fucking funny." He swallows and glares at me. "What's the plan today? We get there, watch you kick ass, come back to my parents and get drunk?"

"Nah, I'm going to go back to my mom's. She's making fideo tonight and I'm not leaving without having a bowl or five."

"No idea what the hell that is but it sounds good, maybe we can come by and—"

I cut Wes off. "You two stay with your parents. I want to spend time with my mom without you being up my ass," I lie.

I'm still reeling from the shit with Ivy, last thing I need to add to my plate is babysitting his ass too. Then there's the issue behind allowing them to see me at my weakest because, let's face it, my mom is the only place where I can crumble into nothing and still be seen as a man. I'm too embarrassed to be like that around Nadia, she needs me strong until she feels safe enough to always be vulnerable with me.

"Boo. Alright though, we need to get to the track."

"That we do," Zap chimes in, whipping his mouth and dropping the napkin on his empty plate. Wes follows suit, then I'm last, sucking down a gulp of my sweet tea. We pay, leaving a few extra ones on the table for a tip, and practically run to the car. As I drive, Zap discusses the other racers and which sponsors will be there. A few I've never heard of, some who are up-and-coming and hunting for the next big hit to line their pockets, then there's the tried and true. Depending on the contracts, I can land a few of them and rake in cash—the ultimate goal.

At the participant gate, we are let in, given my racing number, and directed to a staging area. Some of the drivers came with full trailers loaded with equipment, others like me are here with what they can manage to carry and a few extra hands. We're grouped together, the fame and fortune at the front, the rest of us low-life's at the back. Time is moving at a slow pace to boot, nothing feels real when we begin to set up and do last minute checks.

There are girls everywhere, walking about in their bikini tops and shorts—at least they have sneakers on and not fucking flip flops that will be ruined by the end of the day. Wes makes an occasional side eye but manages to keep quiet and work; one day I'll have the money to pay the both of them well enough where this is all they have to do. Right now, they work because they're my friends and have enough love for me to help and never complain.

I wish Nadia was here. She would love this. Hell, with how responsive she was last night I might even go as far as gearing her up and strapping her into the passenger seat with me every time I have to perform. I can picture her there in a matching riding suit, helmet to keep that pretty head of hers safe, a computer in her lap watching the techy-shit Zap could teach her about. Living in the fast lane with me, one day at a time—the dream.

"Calling all drivers to the starting line. Please have your numbers displayed in the appropriate positions, safety gear on, and be ready to start in twenty minutes."

That's my cue. I step away from the Civic with my leather riding suit hanging low on my hips and a black t-shirt fitting snug but comfortably over my torso and chest. Not my typical getup, I usually prefer my clothes a little more loose and less form fitting—looking like I'm about to go crank out a pump session at the gym rather than drive my ass off in this race. There's a purpose for it though, it makes getting in and out of this track suit easier because I know when I cross that finish line my balls are going to be swimming. If you don't know how difficult it is to get out of one of these when you're drenched, take my word for it, it's pretty similar to peeling off the first layer of skin. Wes, Zap, and I make quick work of my helmet and load up.

Strapping me into the seat, and then some, like I'm about to rocket to the moon. Both of them grab a polyester tongue on both sides of my harness and pull simultaneously; cinching down the belt until it aches. The car may roll but I'm not coming out of this fucker no matter what.

"You ready for this, man?" Wes asks, grabbing my steering wheel and attaching it back onto the steering column with a metallic clink.

"Yeah!" I shout through my helmet, nodding at the same time. Tapping both hands on the wheel, checking that it's secure. Zap is at my other side tucking the fire-retardant lining of my suit into the bottom of my helmet.

"Remember, Grant likes to cut corners sharp so if you plan on catching him in the turns you'll want to swing wide but you'll need more speed. Trevor has a tendency to bully, whatever you do, don't engage with his shit."

I nod. Any other day I'd have an all-out brawl with them, throw fists, black eyes, and break bones. They won't get a rise out of me today, not when my eyes are set on the prize—both of their sponsorships. Nothing says 'fuck you' quite like 'I've taken your money', and coming for it like some bat out of hell.

The door shuts hard next to me, Wes leans over and turns the car on where she rumbles, vibrating through the wheel to my gloves and up my arms. During staging he unhooked everything that may draw power—and though the weight still exists, I should be able to compensate with speed. Therefore, the AC is off and it's hot as fuck in here. He's out seconds later, both of them grabbing the netting installed at both windows to hook them into place, protecting me if either one breaks and caves in or I turn on my side.

I'm set as soon as Zap gives me the thumbs up. When he does, I shift into drive and crawl to the starting line, quickly finding my spot between number sixteen and eighteen. Other drivers and I sit in place, idling, up to the last possible second when another announcement comes from the strategically placed speakers across the property.

"Ladies and gentlemen, drivers and staff, start your engines. The race will commence in two minutes. Any stragglers will be left in the dust and laughed at."

This is it. THE race that seals every deal or breaks every promise.

Both hands squeeze the metal of my replacement wheel, the leather of my gloves creaking from the force. Counting the seconds one by one, then the warning bell chimes at sixty. It's almost showtime. There's not another announcement, we just all prepare for the light to switch. It's a portable traffic light, one sitting on both sides of the roadway, the red gleaming bright and fierce as engines rev, air intakes spew, and every driver sits on the edge of their fucking seats.

"Lose 'em," I hear Nadia's voice in my head.

Mi Diabolica.

Instantly the light swaps from red to green, my left foot slams the clutch to the floor, right hand shifting the Civic into first gear, my right foot hits the accelerator and launches us forward. If I wasn't already cemented to my bucket seat, I'd be thrown back into it with the force I blast off in.

The RPM's hit the red and I shift to second, third, fourth—skirting by cars built to run much faster than my own but driven by guys who can't drive their way out of a paper bag.

Tunnel vision hits and I lose myself in the fury of the race. Dips and curves don't stand a chance, not when each limb moves in synchronicity and Delinquent shows everyone what we're made of. Grant and Trevor are my targets, it's me or them, and I'm not one to let anyone walk all over me on a track.

Ever.

CHAPTER FOURTEEN

W hat a fucking day.

I knew I had it in me, but if you would've told me when I was twelve that I'd be signing sponsor contracts after one of my first major races, I'd have looked at you like you were insane.

All of the stars have aligned this weekend, each of them big ass balls of burning gas in the sky are laid out like a road map for me. Pointing me down the right path at every turn, they even sparkle and cheer for me from thousands of light years away. The professors at school say stars likely died before their light ever made it to Earth but you know what? Who gives a shit, they're dotting the sky like colorless traffic signals and that's good enough for me.

After dropping the boys off, I decided it was time I went for a drive—needing to be alone to process all of the crazy shit that has happened this weekend.

I chose to take the backroads tonight, abandoning the straightaways and interstates, choosing dips and curves over topping out my speed. It's so damn easy to get lost out here, to feel the road hum under the tires, the air whipping through the rolled down windows, and peace.

It took all damn day but I'm finally calm; the threat to Ivy, Gene man-handling Nadia—the anger has passed. I've made a new bed to lie in and I'm going to do it with my chin held high. I refuse to allow the guilt of what I've done bar me from a good damn life with her. Just one more day, one more mass with ma, one more night's rest at home, then I'll have Nadia all to myself.

I'm ready.

Pantera comes over the radio, a little harder than what I normally listen to but this song is a major exception. It's a Black Sabbath remaster and almost as good as the original, so what do I do? Turn it up of course. The autotune and warm pre-summer air steals my voice, my subconscious guiding the car through the woods between gravel roads.

Some of them I take because they're shortcuts that connect to more winding blacktops, others lead me to old stomping grounds that I like to reminisce over. At the back of the Manning property, for example, sits a worn-down cabin the football team used to hang out at and do stupid shit—many times ending with hangovers and a few black eyes. Boys are just as hormonal as the girls, when you pack a bunch of raging guys into a small hut in the middle of bum fuck Egypt, fights ensue. Luckily, I never found myself in one of them because my tastes were more refined than cheerleaders with easy skirts.

Another good spot is the creek running through town where we loved to swim, as long as we went to the north side. The south has more pollution and trash we didn't want to get wrapped up in—no one takes care of things anymore and let it go to hell. One summer I broke my collar bone jumping off of the tire swing that was strung up from a tree that hung over the water. Since then, someone has cut the tire down, preventing kids from having a good and safe time there. It's a bummer really, the more people destroy, the less people have to do and that leads to problems all on their own.

We also used to have a skating rink, I remember going to a birthday party there one year and seeing Nadia with her dad. He had his arm draped over some young girl, saying god knows what, while Nadia zipped around the rink. She fell down and the lacquer covered floor rubbed through her pants and right to the skin where it broke and bled.

Back then, girls were gross. They had germs and if they weren't into boy things I stayed far-far away—my mom was the one who ran over to help pick Nadia up from the floor. She cried and cried, her skinny arms over my mom's shoulders, clinging to her like a Koala bear with her clunky skates tapping my mom's hips. At the benches, they sat down together as my mom consoled her. I stayed away. I kept my distance as I watched ma treat her better than her own flesh and blood ever had; I'm pretty sure that's the day my mom fell for her.

Sometimes I can't believe how entwined our lives are. We've existed at the edge of each other's bubble for the majority of our childhoods, then practically forgot the other existed. Hell, I didn't realize who she was until I brought her home to meet my mom for the first time. It's no secret, my mom was so happy to see her again. She even told us story after story that we shared but couldn't remember. It wasn't too long after that I started dating her, giving her all of the free time left over from football and school—I was wrapped around her fingers then too.

The road I'm on now, Darby Parkway meets Ridge Road at the stop sign coming up. While Darby is nice for unadventurous rides, Ridge is the fun one. It's a blast to drift down, the gravel is never set right which allows the wheels to slide with ease. Each intersection collides with another black top before opening back up to gravel again. I've run up and down this road more times than I can count, if I wanted to I might be able to take it with my eyes closed. Let's be honest though, I'm not the smartest guy but I'm sure as fuck not stupid, it's best to keep my damn peepers open this late in the evening.

I still want to play though.

Pulling onto Ridge, I downshift and gently pick up speed, testing for any grooves that may have been carved into the dirt by heavier trucks—then covered by rock instead of grated and resurfaced, that would make too much sense. When I don't feel any, my speed increases as the first S-curve comes up. Adrenaline pumps rapidly through my veins right as I move into the bend and give the car more gas, throwing her ass out to the right, my hands instinctively counter steering. The second I'm through to the other side, I yank her to the left and repeat, coming out of the curve sideways.

Straightening her up, we take off again. Force from the acceleration digging her tires into gravel and kicking up dust behind us.

Gripping the steering wheel, a laugh bubbles low in my gut—elation. Unbridled joy and excitement in doing my favorite fucking thing. A sharp C-curve is coming up next. I'll need to hug the inside of the turn without letting the wheels slide off the road, a challenge I always found terrifying but have conquered many times over.

Flicking the brights on, the headlights illuminate everything several yards ahead of me—ensuring the way is clear. Trees no longer shroud the roads edge in bleak shadows; no, the proverbial red carpet has been laid out and is waiting for me to burn rubber down it. Right as the angle of the road begins to dip, Delinquent finds her own rhythm and pushes her nose deep into the curve as I press on the gas.

Crunching and rasping gravel groans outside of my lowered window, the slide so damn smooth I don't think I've ever felt anything like it. Almost as buttery as driving over sand and having the shifty ground anchor you into place through the remainder of the turn. Emerging from the curve, Ridge opens up straight where I can gun it again. A plume of dust and debris flying into the air behind me the faster I go—leaving a trail, no my mark, carving my name and existence into a world far too busy to notice a regular fuck like me.

I can only imagine what the future holds, what changes and events will take place as I grow older and live the life I tailor made. Too many times I catch myself dreaming about all of the things I'll get to do when my career takes off, the experiences. How society will shift, advances in technology, healthcare, war and government, everything. Hell, even when I inevitably change. Then throw Nadia into the mix with me? I can't wait, let me get home, get off this fucking road and sleep so I can rush through tomorrow and race back to her.

Working through several more turns, Ridge begins to straighten out and lose its edge. One short stint, then another, until they start elongating the further I get around Hazelwood like a halo—or bullseye depending on how you look at things. The ground transitions easily to half rock and half blacktop. Delinquents weight and speed disrupts the earth beneath the roads edges, causing them to crumble and fall away a little at a time, adding to the normal erosion. Cheap towns and counties refusing to fix roads less traveled, like these, in this very condition. Hazardous as they may be, we still drive down the damn things. Were it me managing the budget,

Ridge would be in tiptop shape all year round, just so I can spend nights like these cruising up and down it without a care in the world.

A field opens up to my left, the home of millions and millions of yellow cone flowers and the critters that hide within the stems and grass. Their sweet scent floats through the open cab, a too-bright moon lighting up the inside of the car as it spills unapologetically through the windshield. On the outskirts of the pasture sits a protective border of metal cattle bar to keep trespassers off grazing land, which has since emptied with the death of farming.

Resting my right hand on the gearshift, the left controlling the steering wheel, I relax into the rest of my drive. Nadia's memory sits next to me in the passenger seat, where she belongs, and teases me with faint whiffs of her body spray. All of it, the road, the sky, her phantom, drapes me with a warm sort of comfort and ease as if she's reaching through space and time to slide her hand to brace and squeeze my shoulder. Warmth blooming at where I picture her touch. It's simple and platonic, contrasting every other thought I have about her, but it works—it feels good. Before I know it, it's traveling through my chest and coiling around my heart, creeping up to my mind where I need nothing but her.

"One last curve, baby. Let's get through it and get out of here."

Whitesnake is carrying the both of us now, the upbeat tune causing me to press harder on the gas pedal. I can't end this ride without one more adrenaline pumping drift.

"Keep on pushing, babe. Like I've never known before. You know you drive me crazy—take me down slow and easyyyy." David Coverdale sings, right as I hit the turn.

Grabbing the e-brake, I give it a slight yank, and let off the gas. Delinquent soars through the turn perfectly. We're almost out when the gravel shifts and catches the front passenger tire—jerking the car and ripping us out of sync. Releasing the brake, I grab the wheel and correct the turn, muscles in my biceps burn the harder I pull it to the left. Sending my stomach into my throat and my pulse through the roof.

The car squirrels around some, overcorrecting to the left. Pulling the wheel to the right, the biggest fucking mistake of my life happens when I push on the brake. Delinquent jerks straight but it's too late, another rock-covered groove snags the wheel and all control is lost.

The moon darkens, shadows swallowing both me and the car in an unforgiving gulp a split second before the crunch of metal deafens my left and shattering glass cuts me with hundreds of tiny shards.

Everything goes quiet when a beautifully broken pair of tear-filled silver eyes splinter my heart in two, with a haunting rattle clinging to one more silent word.

Nadia.

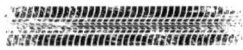

"What's your name, Diabolica?"

She scowls, hands instantly finding and shoving at my chest—her enthusiasm barely ruffling the buttery-leather of my worn-out jacket. When I don't release her, the coaches scraping her victim off the floor to our left, she softens. Inhaling the longest calming breath I've ever seen.

"Nadia."

"It's nice to meet you. I'm Kaleb Reyes."

With a mind of its own, my right thumb brushes her cheek. She sure is pretty.

"I know."

Those two words are all it takes for the whole world to fall away—she knows me. Internally, I kick myself in the ass for not having noticed her before. Perhaps it's the unflattering clothing she wears, or how she doesn't belong to the same scene as other girls do; at least those that vie for male attention. Maybe she just doesn't care to stick out, other than when her fist fights draw attention from the whole damn cafeteria.

"I've seen you around school a couple times. I don't think we've ever had any electives together." *I lie, hoping to dig and encourage her to share a bit more.*

My hold falls and my hands go ice-cold when she pulls away—no longer there to keep them warm.

"We haven't had any."

"No? Hmm, we must have friends in common. That means, by proxy, we're friends now."

"Hardly."

A full playful smile blooms on my face at her retort. This girl, she's something else. Any other time they're fawning over me, fighting against the grain to maintain my attention, but not her. Noooo, not this walking billboard of trust issues and a bad attitude. She's practically blowing me off as I stand here, and I sure as hell can't have that. Nadia goes to step away, the student body splitting like something out of the Bible as more teachers arrive, but I move quickly to block her escape.

"I like the sound of that. We're hardly friends—we're besties now."

"Over my dead body," *she nearly growls.*

"I prefer you alive and trying to scratch my eyes out."

"Oh man, you know what, you're right. I exist solely because you wish me alive."

Good god she's quick. Stubborn as an ox but that's okay, it keeps me on my toes and I do love a challenge.

"Go with me to the game tonight."

"Are you asking me, or telling me?" She turns to me, a little dumbfounded at my sudden advance.

"Telling." My teeth capture my bottom lip as I smirk down at her. I can't help but note how gorgeous her eyes are when she tilts her head back to stare—no glare—at me with an arched brow.

"Aren't you playing?"

"Mm, yeah, but I can make time to come see you in the stands."

Nadia steps closer, our bodies nearly touch as she reaches out and fumbles the zipper pulley on my jacket—my breath hitches. She's silent for two, four, five seconds before hitting me in the pride with her vicious mouth.

"No thanks, football is boring. All you do is wear spandex and touch each other's ass."

Huffing at her, a wedge of cafeteria air forms a buffer between her, and if I'm not mistaken, a little annoyance.

"Now wait a damn minute."

"Pierce, my office. Now!" Mr. Trenton orders from the hallway leading to his dungeon, his hands resting on his hips as he looks at her disapprovingly.

"See you later—bestie." She teases, then kills me with a playful wink.

Hazelwood Gazette

MAN KILLED IN AN AUTO CRASH ON NOTORIOUSLY UNSAFE ROAD

Kaleb Alejandro Reyes, 21, of 1725 Flower Pass Rd, was pronounced dead at the scene at 10:25 p.m., by local authorities Saturday night.

The accident occurred around 9:50 p.m., north of Route 78, off of Ridge Rd, when Reyes lost control of his vehicle after passing over unsafe road conditions and crossing southbound. Skid marks stretching across both lanes show the path Reyes's car took before it slid off the roadway and into the tree line.

Upon exiting, Reyes's car collided with trees before coming to an abrupt stop several meters away. His automobile was reported as crushed, killing Reyes on impact.

Police discovered a damaged b[...] line and determined the fin[...] were normal wear and tear; al[...] of foul play. In addition, no [...] injuries or property damage [...] sustained at the time of [...] accident.

Reyes was a graduate [...] Hazelwood High, and a stude[...] Michigan State University. Fu[...] services will be held at 2:30 [...] Sunday at the St. Gabriel Ca[...] Church in Nottingham.

IF YOU WOULD LIKE [...] DONATE TO FUNERA[...] PROCEEDINGS OR T[...] BURIAL FOR MR. REY[...] PLEASE CONTACT S[...] GABRIEL CHURCHE[...] ADMINISTRATOR[...] MONDAY THROUG[...] FRIDAY.

Epilogue One

Babalon - Chapter Two

Nadia

I'm drowning.

An ache is squeezing the air from lungs so hard they're going to burst. Each constriction prevents the next strangled gasp from filling them. They're raw, full of agony and the remnants of my screamed pleas. Sorrow filled tears drip heavily down my face, leaving my eyes red-rimmed despite not having any more left to give.

This is the hell I've been living in for days, since I walked away from his lowered casket and the sound of his family's cries. The text I received from Mama Reyes was a shock, but things didn't truly set in until I had to look at him at the funeral home. When I got word of the newspaper article, I ran to the closest gas station to find one. The ghost of sharp gravel digging into my knees still haunts me—seeing the mangled mess of his car on the front page, through the dispenser's glass, dropped me to the pavement.

Shaking, I pressed the button and pulled the door open to drag out over twenty pages of extra nonsense just to read the article more clearly. Tears fell over my cry-pinkend cheeks, dripping onto and soaking into the thin paper. There in black and white, listed the details of his wreck. Of the time, the place, and how he was dead on impact.

My heart neared implosion, painful pressure so heavy on my chest, I couldn't breathe through the agony. Every aspect of his accident filtered through my thoughts in wave after wave of 'what if's' and 'why's'.

Did he panic and over-correct? Was he under the influence after his race? Did he accept his fate when the edge of the road yanked his car further away? What was going through his mind in those last seconds before the lights went out and his heart stopped? Is the seven seconds real? Did his short life flash before his eyes and he got to experience all the greatest moments one last time?

Death is surreal to think about. One second the person you love the most is standing next to you, dragging you into their arms refusing to let you go. Promising to take you away from the existence you've known all your life, then the next they're gone. The humor and relief they brought to your life, the love and happiness suddenly over. Late nights lying across the hood of his car will never happen again. Tucked away in the back seat, listening to his heart thump against my ear and the low melody of his rock music cocooning us...I will never have that with him again.

He will never get to race under any labels or contracts. His dreams and goals ending on the side of the road, alone, and it breaks my heart knowing he passed away without those he loved most next to him.

I was on the verge of losing my own will to live when I showed up at the funeral home, his mom and sisters huddled together in the front row of pews. His two friends sitting behind them with their hands on Mama Reyes's shoulder while sucking down their own tears. There I was, feeling like an outsider to their love.

He was surrounded by candles and offerings, an ofrenda put up towards the foot of his casket, photos of Mother Mary, flowers, plants, what broke me the most was his leather jacket draped over the top and his keys. I couldn't do it, walk up and see him, touch his hand and cry over his body like others have because if I did they'd have to put me in a fucking asylum.

I let my best friend go that day and I haven't been the same since. He's been gone a few years now and I've wallowed in my sorrow long enough. There's no limit to grief, there's no right or wrong way to process it either, but I'm ready. I need to move on and stop letting it have dominion over me. I need to find something that gives me purpose so I can, at minimum, make it to the next sunrise because if I'm being honest, I don't want to live.

I came home about twenty minutes ago and locked myself in my room still reeking of an innocent girl—and I'm far from one. I've been damaged in ways that would damage normal families. Betrayed by everyone I've ever known, then left behind when I should have been in the passenger seat next to Kaleb.

Part of me knows I would have survived the wreck if I was with him and lived through a different type of regret and grief. Maybe it would have been easier to come to terms with his death if I was there. For the rest of my life, I will want to call and hope he picks up his phone where I can hear his warm voice on the other end. That infectious smile he had, his playful jabbing, his love.

Last night's shift was uneventful at best. Working multiple jobs is taking a toll on me physically, adding to the mental load I've carried around for years. I'm ready for a break. As soon as I came in, I booted up my computer to begin looking through online classifieds for something more. The main goal is to leave Hazelwood, if I'm able to combine my pay from all of my jobs into one and relocate—yeah, that would help me the most.

Finding a posting for a Basic Correctional Officer, I skimmed the qualifications and noticed it came with continuing education—making me think of Kaleb and what he said about college not being what it's cracked up to be. Researching this though, it's much shorter—not requiring four years and countless hours only for a piece of paper at the end. It has structure, classroom time, and physical training; set up more like a job rather than school

Can I do this? Look criminals in the face every day without being so damn angry at the world I take it out on them? Can I finally heal?

Hovering my mouse over the 'apply' button, I finally click and the screen changes to one with spots vacantly waiting for my information. I still smell like ass from my shift, clothes stained with mysterious substances I choose to avoid rather than stripping away and diving headfirst into the shower.

This...it can't wait. I need an escape, I need out of this place.

My eyes run like faucets, always crying or raw from doing so. Right now they're welled with tears again but I blink them away, determined to get through this application. My fingers fly across the keyboard, filling in the information one box at a time—focused and detailed in what I'm providing. Will I be qualified enough to bring in for an interview? Who knows, but I'm going to try regardless of the outcome.

This could be my chance out of Hazelwood. As much as I would like to call it quits on life itself, just disappear instead of putting my heart and soul through the pieces of a tortured life, I can't. Not when Kaleb would want more for me, let's not forget he'd be at my shoulder telling me what to put in each space to make me a more favorable candidate.

Somewhere out there, there's more for me and I want to find it—love, maybe a family. Something equally mine as it is someone else's. Kaleb wouldn't have wanted me to give up and even though I don't want to keep going some nights, I have to do it for him. I have to take him with me even if it's only in my heart. Road trips, exploring the world, experiencing things we have only dreamt of seeing. Getting married, building my family however I wish. Loud music, louder cars, and long night drives.

Page after page goes by before I reach the end, hitting submit like I'm smashing the launch button for the country's nukes—the answer to all of my problems. For a moment power surges through me—I'm taking control and don't care who's here to see it.

This is *my* life and if I have my way, it will be as wild as that last ride he promised me.

Epilogue Two

Babalon – Chapter Twenty-Five

Kaleb

The second she sparked my lighter I felt my soul drawn from the blinding bliss of the afterlife to the stench of her childhood home. Laden with anger, disgust, and a sorrow so deep in the wood paneling they're warping.

Her room is utterly destroyed. The window I used to sneak in and out of is coated in a foggy film blocking the once clear view, then the blankets she had pinned over the filthy glass now ripped and torn into shreds. Her bed, dresser, desk, it's all demolished too. Someone came in here in a frenzy, damaging everything they could to make a statement and it's so fucking loud it's nearly screaming with resentment.

I used to spend hours in here under her touch, wearing goofy-looking beauty masks and creams I'd let her paint across my skin. Listening to her babble on and on about something she learned in school that day—she was always a go-getter, aiming for the damn stars even with a ball and chain anchoring her to this hell hole.

Like everything else in her life, those incredible memories are now tarnished by filth. Whoever did this is showing her how little she means to them—and I have an idea who.

I begin to dwell, to fume over her fathers hatred when she catches my eye. Snapping my gaze to her, I'm across the room in a flash, idling behind her as pure energy and nothing more.

Sliding her hand into her jeans, she leaves the lighter there and sighs in disappointment. Instinctively I reach to soothe her, hooking my hand into the crook of her arm only for her to pass right through me like I'm made of fog.

Squeezing my fist, every breath of my soul wishes to feel the warmth of her body; the smooth skin I used to pepper kisses across, the soft areas where I would sink my teeth into her. Breaks my heart everytime I do this, you would think I'd have learned my lesson by now, that I'll never feel her skin against mine again and she will only ever sense me rather than hear me or see my face.

Fuck, I miss her.

Following her out of her room, I'm struck by how run down her home is. He let this place go to shit when she left—I shouldn't be surprised, he's always been a disgusting pig, it's still jarring. When we enter the living area, there's more. Fucker is bordering on a hoarder type situation where there's more trash blanketing most of the surfaces including the asshole-garbage man himself. Gene, hunkered at his old chair rolling a cigarette with a very noticeable tremble in his hands. Desperate for a hit of nicotine he doesn't look up when Nadia enters, ignoring her like he always has unless he needs something.

While I sympathize, the way Nadia disregards him tells me every-thing—she's cut him out and deservingly so. Observing every ounce of anger and hatred in the move she makes, I linger in the shadows with my arms crossing my chest, expecting her to put that wrath to use.

My face lights up when she pulls the Zippo from her pocket and strikes it, the few metal snicks giving way to a flame she stares at for a few beets, watching the flame dance in her hand. She's mesmerized, I'm not sur-prised, the way she threw the molotov cocktail at a damn cop? Kinda set her up, you know? Maybe it's that night she thinks of, she finds happiness in flames, because she thinks of me—let's hope it's that.

Nadia's hand waves under the dingy curtains hanging over the living room windows. Allowing the flames to lick at them when she's done getting lost in the orange glow, her dad not paying her a bit of attention while she silently sets them on fire.

I remember the day she hung them, I was camped out in her room, jacket hung on the back of her desk chair and sprawled across her twin sized bed when he came home, shouting for her from the kitchen. At first I didn't want her to leave, to pretend she was asleep, but we both knew better. He would have hunted her down and found me in the process. Despite hating him, she responded to his every beck and call, it was better she went—always better to avoid the confrontation with him rather than duke it out.

She returned an hour later, he sat in his chair while she did all the work, watching a fucking football game between the Raiders and the Cowboys—*thrilling game*. He made no attempt to help her, no direction, opinion, and even made her find the tools all on her own. Of course, in the end, they were hung up with the right equipment while the ones in her room were pinned by thumb-tacks.

The good mood she had was gone when she returned to me. I sensed her tension when the door clicked closed with a soft snick—trying to shrink away from the man who gave her life.

That day was a turning point for her. She was already retreating from him, from her friends, and doing the bare minimum outside of protecting them. At times I would give her a ride to Ivy or Wren's place but she'd call me again in the middle of the night to come get her, and I never protested. I always hated bringing her back here but where else could she go? My mom would expect more than what either of us were ready for if she woke up the next morning and Nadia was tucked away in my bed. Her dad would also come looking if he woke up and she was missing—bet you money he would have called the cops and Uncle would have been the first dickhead to show up at our door.

Now that she's on her own, capable, and fighting for herself instead of others, I pray that this is the last time she will ever come back here. I hope she burns every fucking thing in this house to ash and finally turns her back on the man she desperately tried to love who never wanted her to begin with—only wanted to hurt her mom.

Observing the filthy curtains catching fire more quickly, I grin. This is what she needs—to burn away memories that bring her pain and heartache. There was a time where self-hatred burdened her and now that she's taking matters into her own hands, I couldn't be more proud. It took her long enough but sometimes you can't rush perfection.

Nadia moves over to the other set of curtains when her dad finally realizes what's happening and freaks out, rushing to the kitchen to grab the expired fire extinguisher he stuffed under the sink fifteen years ago. Pulling the pin, he squeezes the handle and sweeps the nozzle side to side only for nothing to spray from the dusty tip. His anger goes nuclear, screaming and shouting all while my girl sets more shit on fire.

There's no stopping me, even as a damn ghost she turns me on and I need to touch her. At her back, I lean in and kiss the side of her neck. Amazed when the skin there prickles with goosebumps—the chill of my existence contrasting the sweltering heat of a house ablaze.

"Get out of the house before you're joining me on this side. You have far too much to live through before it's time to be in my hands again." I whisper at the soft skin behind her ear.

Pocketing my Zippo again, she uses her free hand to rub her neck where my lips skimmed just seconds ago.

That's right, I'm still here. I'm always here.

I'm hovering over her like an ominous cloud when we get outside. If I were alive, I'd be pressed to her side, breathing down into the mess of dark locks she calls hair. Listening to the crackling roar of an inferno to my left, the wailing of a fire truck too wide to fit through the road-parked cars, and her father's nerve grating voice.

"Nadia?"

Hearing her name being called, I turn in sync with her, protective even now when a stranger approaches. He's a well put together man—slacks, button up, smooth combed hair. Not her taste, by far.

I wonder who the fuck this cat is.

"Detective. Wasn't aware IA dabbled in accidental fires."

"Mm, that's why I am here. The fire marshal said this may be arson according to the homeowner."

I can't help being nosey and listening to their conversation, the weight of the afterlife pulling at me with its chains and ropes—almost time to return to the fray. I've visited briefly a time or two in the past few years and will make it a point to come around again, but the pressure grows the longer I'm here.

Wishing I could interrupt her conversation and tell her goodbye, promise I'll come back, I hope deep in her heart she feels me, and knows how proud of her I am.

Proud is an understatement. She deserves this. Freedom.

Mi cosita diabolica.

Bonus Chapter

*We're just two lost souls swimming in a fishbowl, year after year. Running
over the same old ground, what have we found?
The same old fears, wish you were here*
-Pink Floyd

Nadia

Perfect weather; it's few and far between but sometimes you're blessed
with days like today. Kace and I drove back to Michigan this week for
nothing other than this—me laying here in the tall grass, flowers protrud-
ing high above my prone body, and the velvety rays of sun cast across my
limbs. The foliage is vibrant green, the sky is the clearest and most pure
blue I've seen in weeks, and I'm cocooned in silence—in my own world
devoid of life's chaotic messes.

That's pretty much all there is in a cemetery, as one would guess. There
are rows and rows of headstones, monuments, mausoleums, decorated by
loved ones and the occasional sniffling sound of pain joined with the trees'

rustling leaves. It's calm and heartbreaking all at once; the most beautiful part of home, as morbid as that sounds.

While I'm not here for pain's sake, I'm here for him—Kaleb.

I haven't come to visit since his casket was lowered into the ground and dirt was thrown over the top. Feels like a lifetime ago and, if I'm honest, it almost is. Sadie is about to graduate college and before I can give her the graduation gift of a lifetime, in my opinion, I had to get his blessing.

Rolling onto my side, I look into the deep green blades of grass covering Kaleb's grave—where I like to believe he's lying next to me. Staring warmly into my now aged-silver eyes. Matching the smile I have smeared across my face as we silently share what's happened through our lives—since the day he was laid to rest. Truthfully, I haven't said anything for the hour I've been laying here, too content in the blanket of warmth and love I still feel for him.

This wasn't how it was supposed to be, we were meant to escape and live long boring lives: football practice, PTO meetings, barbecues on the weekends, and Christmas gatherings with torn wrapping paper to the ceiling. What we had back then was young, wild, and free but the most painful part was that I didn't know what I had until it was gone.

If you're asking where Kace is, he's giving me the time and space I need, standing by the car instead of hovering like he's prone to doing nowadays. This conversation is between Kaleb and I, my grand idea, to share news and hunt for some sort of sign he's still with me. I'm just too scared to have it, what if he thinks this is me saying goodbye forever? What if I'm overthinking this shit and need to pull my panties out of my ass and get on with the show?

"Babygirl?" Kace's rough voice picks up behind me. Carrying on the wind like some sort of weighted blanket ready to drape over me if my mind forms another small fissure and sends me into an emotional spiral.

I am so fucking in love with him it's disgusting, then I confess, at times it's unfathomably beautiful. We're broken, amazing, and infatuated with one another. Our road was long and challenging but time won out and we learned that despite the absolute hell life put us through, nothing will break us. The love I feel for him is incomparable to anything I've felt before, including the love I have for Kaleb—it's just different. Kace filled in the gaps I had cracking my heart into pieces, Kaleb taught me it was safe to let someone love me enough to fill them in.

Sighing through the weight of being at his gravesite, I draw in a deep lungful of wildflower and spring-time air. Over my shoulder, wind ruffles his hair when I give him a rueful smile he stops in his track, shoving his hands in the pockets of his jeans. He doesn't move closer. Watching me from a few yards away still as dumbfounded as the first day he really saw me. He remains where he's at, watching me with those mismatched eyes of his. He's afraid I'll fall apart sitting here, not metaphorically either, the man is practically waiting to see my seams unravel and for me to crumble but I'm alright.

His heart is so full for me and our children; protective, attentive, everything neither one of us had growing up. He's the best husband and father I could have ever begged for—for family. The days he gets a hair up his ass, I promptly remind him that it's us in this family, not just him and his fear; the better part of both of our lives may have dissolved into years of agony but tomorrow will be better.

"I'm alright," I answer before he has the chance to ask.

Placing my hands on the firm ground, I push against it to lift myself up, small pebbles and bits of dust biting into my palms as I sit myself up. Another slight gust of wind catches my hair right as I'm finding my footing and straightening up. The way my heart lurches, looking directly at Kaleb's slowly withering headstone, makes me nauseous years later.

He needs a new one but I don't want to touch it without his mama's permission. Maybe, before we leave, I can stop by and see her for a moment and ask her about getting him one that will better withstand the elements and time. It would be really good to catch up with her too, as long as I don't have to run into her brother again. I've not seen him since my ride from Darkwater to jail—Officer Reyes—and I would like to keep it that way. He barely remembered me but that little bit was enough to sting in the back of the cop car. I've also caught a few whispers about him over the years but chose to ignore them along with everything else I couldn't change.

Running my fingertips through the lettering—*Friend & Son*—I try my damndest not to smirk but it's impossible when I feel just as close to him today as I did when we last rode together.

"You know, this was supposed to go a different way. You were supposed to be here with me so we could tear up the roads and run Hazelwood ragged with our shit. Life turned out a whirlwind, that's for sure, but I wish you were here. Out of all of it, I wanted you to see what I've finally accomplished—husband, daughter...a son."

Yes.

I'm pregnant again and high-risk due to my *advanced age*. Kace and I found out a few months ago; we're too excited to do things right this time around. We get the chance to do the things we missed with Sadie, then she also gets another person who will think she hung the moon, just like her father and I. Which is part of why I am here.

"Think I could get your mom to change your headstone to *'god father'*? That'd be pretty bad ass. We could dress up like mafia families on Halloween for his birthday to come see you if you'd like."

I chuckle at the absurd idea—Kaleb would love that though. Maybe I should tell Kace so he can start planning which family we will portray every year until our little boy grows out of it.

Reaching, I comb back a lock of hair and pin it behind my ear when I crouch down and press my forehead to the top of his headstone.

"For a few weeks I struggled with the perfect name but I finally found it and before I tell anyone else, I wanted to tell you. At first I thought Kace was going to fight me on it, but that son of a bitch really has the biggest damn heart I've ever seen."

Kace starts up the car at that moment—Kaleb's. I bought it, correction...Kace did, and we've spent almost every day in the garage rebuilding it from the ground up. I was surprised mama Reyes still had it; grateful too. Had I been in her shoes, I may have blamed the car and scraped it. I understand why she kept it though, after clearing out his dorm room, it's all she had left of her little boy and now that I'm pregnant with one of my own? I get it.

We decided to drive it to see Kaleb's grave, homage in a way. What better way to return to where it all began than in the one and only *Delinquent*. Hell, I can promise anyone that he's smiled down from the sky when she rumbled through the gate to the cemetery.

"Kaleb Elijah Patton. Has a ring to it, don't you think?" I finally squeeze out, because as happy as I am about redoing parenthood, it still hurts saying his name.

Hearing the sound of the car rev, I look back over my shoulder at Kace when he unfolds his big ass from the driver seat and shuts the door. She's beautiful—Delinquent–black on black, just like he had her back in the day. I've added a few mods since, making sure she can drift and clear corners in no time flat, he'd want her that way.

Following Kace as he approaches, he slides his hand around my lower back, leans in to kiss my temple where a few silver-streaked strands catch in his five o'clock shadow.

"You ready to go? I don't want to rush you but we have a few more stops to make before we get back. Sadie is also blowing your phone up asking when we are going to be home. Worried we are going to miss her graduation."

"Yeah—I'm about ready. Not that I'd ever miss hers. I know how it feels."

"Come on then. Let's get going. You tell him?"

"Of course I did."

"And? Did you get the reaction you were searching for?"

"Well…I was telling him right as you started the car. That's good enough reaction for me. I know somewhere out there, he's knuckle bumping Ken Brock and sliding into another, ready for one more ride."

Kace

She doesn't look for signs.

171

Bullshit.

Back in the day, Nadia didn't look for signs from the universe but now she waits for them to appear like she can't move on without something acknowledging her. I know it comes from a place of abandonment—first her mom, father...me. I still kick myself in the ass over it, years later, but this is who she is now. It's in her bones.

Brushing my thumb along the soft skin of her mid back, I look at her before turning to peer at her friend's headstone. Sexy fucking thing's wearing a crop top and high-rise shorts. She likes to say it holds in her stomach—rounding with my kid—but I like to believe she wears get-ups like this because it drives me fucking insane. Exactly how I envision her twenty years ago.

The girl Kaleb knew.

Chuckling at her, I nod to the car.

"Go on, I'm on your heels."

The damn woman takes my breath away when she leans over and kisses the top of Kaleb's headstone—I hope the day I die...she worships me the same way. Don't get me wrong, I don't feel an ounce of jealousy but the devotion and love she has rivals anything I've ever experienced growing up.

Nadia moseys to the car, picks up her phone. I assume she's calling Sadie back as she sinks into the passenger seat. I love my daughter, she's as damaged as the rest of us and needs copious amounts of reassurance—which I've learned comes from her time with the Wilsons. Hearing Nadia's few words, promising we will be back in time for her graduation, I turn to Kaleb and touch where Nadia's lips just pressed. Not to wipe it clean, no. To make that sentiment permanent.

"I don't know what you did to make her the way she is but thank you. I know deep in my bones, you were the one who carried her through all the shit she experienced. The other friends she had? Good riddance; fucking hate that she was the glue for that group, and the one with any sort of loyalty."

Nadia's voice carries over the field followed by a slow laugh, and I go quiet–the sound music to my soul.

I continue.

"I never was a spiritual man but once upon a time I begged the lord to let me stay on this Earth. To give me another chance at life so I could return to her and finish what you started."

Snorting lowly, my hand falls back to my side and stuffs into my pockets again as I prepare my own goodbyes to the man who gave me my wife.

"Took me too fucking long, but I'm here now. I promise I'll keep her safe. Thank you for having her back when I didn't, for carrying her through the worst years of her life, and never letting her give up on love. Without you, I never would have met her nor would I have my family—their lives over ours."

The End

Be sure to check out the Lito Duet for Kace & Nadia's story!

ABOUT THE AUTHOR

Thank you for reading *You Wound Me*!

I'm originally from east Texas but have since moved to the greater DFW area after marrying this weird-ass biker guy. Totes tho, he's pretty cool—makes me tacos, tells me I'm pretty. We got hitched on June 21, 2024–my dad's birthday, the summer solstice, and funny enough a full moon; for all my witchy folks out there.

In December 2024, I graduated with my Master's degree in Criminology specialization in Homeland Security, which has fueled my love of writing dark romance centered around Law Enforcement and the legal system. In Late April 2025, I left my job as a Security Supervisor and migrated into the Correctional system following the release of Babalon. With my work experience, and my formal education into criminology, I bring an educated & experienced standpoint to my romance niche. I use this to highlight the good, the bad, and the ugly of life, love, and the legal system.

I take immense pride in what I do, both in and out of the romance novel world, and cannot wait to bring more dark, heart wrenching, and twisted stories to your shelves. The future is already looking pretty bright with several series in the early planning stages and a universe dedicated solely to little ol' me. Let's just say, if you have a uniform kink, then the Darkwater Correctional universe is where you want to be!

Published books
Babalon & Judas - The Lito Duet
You Wound Me

Upcoming books
Sotiras Duet
The Colony Carnivale
New Series

Socials & Website
www.alairnovak.com
IG : @alair_novak
Threads : @alair_novak
Lemon8 : @alair_novak
Tiktok : @alairnovak
Pinterest : @AlairNovak
Bsky : @alairnovak.bsky.social
Neptune : @alairnovak
Facebook : @authoralairnovk

www.ingramcontent.com/pod-product-compliance
Lightning Source LLC
Chambersburg PA
CBHW071436260626
47170CB00008B/2733